Celina
or
the Cats

Celina

or

the Cats

By Julieta Campos

Translated by
Leland H. Chambers

Latin American Literary Review Press
Series: Discoveries
Pittsburgh, Pennsylvania
1995

The Latin American Literary Review Press publishes Latin American creative writing under the series title *Discoveries*, and critical works under the series title *Explorations*.

Library of Congress Cataloging-in-Publication Data
Campos, Julieta.
    [Celina o los gatos. English]
    Celina or the cats / by Julieta Campos; translated by Leland H. Chambers and Kathleen Ross.
    p. cm.--(Discoveries)
    ISBN 0-935480-72-2
    I. Chambers, Leland H., 1928- . II. Ross, Kathleen.
III. Title. IV. Series.
IN PROCESS
863--dc20   95-21118
                                  CIP

Cover art by Lisette Miller. Book design by Suzanne Bryla.

The paper used in this publication meets the minimum requirements of the American National Standard for Permanence of Paper for Printed Library Materials Z39.48-1984 ∞

Celina or The Cats may be ordered directly from the publisher:

Latin American Literary Review Press
121 Edgewood Avenue • Pittsburgh, PA 15218
Tel (412) 371-9023 • Fax (412) 371-9025

ACKNOWLEDGMENTS

This project is supported in part by grants from the National Endowment for the Arts in Washington, D.C., a federal agency, and the Commonwealth of Pennsylvania Council on the Arts.

"The House," translated by Kathleen Ross, *Scents of Wood and Silence: Short Stories by Latin American Woman Writers*, ed. by Kathleen Ross and Yvette E. Miller (Latin American Literary Review Press: Pittsburgh, 1991).

"All the Roses," translated by Leland H. Chambers, *Anaïs: An International Journal*, 13 (1995).

Contents

It is not by accident that I have decided to give this book a title which is also that of one of the stories brought together here. I wanted to dedicate the others to those ambiguous creatures who are always so close to what is enigmatic and hence to poetry. I think all the stories in some measure share in the disturbing, imprecise nature of cats; in each one persists a world that is not resigned to perish, although there is something within that is subtly eating away at it and breaking it down. The order in which the stories appear corresponds to that ever more evanescent form which nonetheless never quite manages to vanish altogether. The characters gradually fade away until there remains only the atmosphere that has accommodated them, empty of voices and expression: the city--one and multiple, echo and nostalgia, a distant irony that rejects those who dwell there.

It seems to me that it is no longer possible to conceive of an author who is not also, to some degree, his own proper critic. I hope that this justifies the above words, and that our epoch's own enthusiasm for erudition, which sometimes seeks ancient rationalizations to give support to its profoundest delusions, may perhaps explain the ones that follow.

FOR ENRIQUE

On Cats and
Other Worlds

*C*ats are those soft, rippling, cruel, delicate beings, those solitary, nocturnal, always unpredictable beings that inject our everyday world with the sphere of the unknown. Other worlds are by their very nature indescribable—those secret, incomprehensible spaces our world denies in order to reassure itself concerning its own invulnerability within the four sheltering walls of a small, domestic, unsurprising universe. How, then, to attempt to circumscribe a theme that is so evasive, slippery, and esoteric?

With its two forefeet supported by a tree trunk with bark almost stripped away and an autumn-yellowed crown that is receiving the drops from a rain-shower pouring out of a single, slightly menacing storm cloud in the upper surface of the painting, a cat of fern stares at us with pupils that are green and motionless. Remedios Varo's fern cat shares the vegetal, passive, receptive, feminine nature of those plants that proliferate in dampness and shadow and spread like mushrooms, moss, and every other species of parasitical vegetation. Octavio Paz has said that Remedios Varo does not paint the world inside out but the world's inner side, and it is exactly this inner side of the world that is suggested by the cat's stare from the abyss. When fantasy appears in daily life the cats circle around. They are our contact with all that is imaginary, indecipherable, unfathomable, inaccessible. That is why there are so many cats within the precincts of fabulous speculation that Remedios Varo leaves ajar for us. Cats of dry leaves, hybrid cats part woman and part owl, cats leaping suddenly up on the tablecloth and introducing disorder, cats interjecting a strange, fantasmagoric air into closed rooms, cats that through an odd electrical agency shoot sparks when petted, cats that poke their heads out of open holes in the floor, cats that come from somewhere else God knows where, watching us with a stare coming from a place outside the painting and even outside the world, coming from the beginning of creation, with the impassiveness of a sphinx.

Obsession with time, presence of the immemorial, of the ancient, of the dawn of consciousness and the end of all things. Privileged witnesses of life and death.

The cat the Egyptians pick up from the banks of the Nile in order to tame it is a talisman, a magical instrument, a vehicule for the taming of the other world. Reducing it to a state of domesticity means domesticating an animal that symbolizes the beyond, darkness, mystification. Later on, turned into the negation of that mystery, the Great Cat Ra kills the dragon/serpent that symbolizes darkness. Feline figures slip around silently in paintings as if walking on velvet, tense and sensitive as the most delicate of instruments, capable of vibrating at the least stimulus. The cat is the favorite animal of those beings who pay tribute to death in order to secure eternal life and bring the passage of time to a halt forever. When Voltaire wrote in the *Philosophical Dictionary* that the abode of the gods was empty of cats, the celestial, imaginary worlds of H. P. Lovecraft had not yet been populated with them. But one must reproach Voltaire with ignorance of the Egyptian pantheon: there the cat is identified with the Moon goddess, wife of the god Ra, and in the temple where the statue of the nocturnal divinity has a feline head, cats abound whose postures and movements assist the priests in delivering their auguries. As the protective spirits of the home, their presence was venerated, and their death provoked sorrow and mourning by the families, who would have them embalmed and buried in their own sepulchres or in cemeteries that had been especially dedicated to these animals. The worship of cats was so deeply rooted among the ancient Egyptians that on one occasion, so goes the legend, Cambyses, the astute monarch of Persia, caused the defeat of the Egyptian army by releasing a great number of cats onto the battlefield between the armies, and the Eyptian warriors were so afraid of committing the crime of shedding the sacred feline blood that they held off from fighting altogether.

Messengers, intermediaries, transmitters of a subterranean current that is trying to sift through to the surface, cats are also closely related, we must not forget, to those other animals the panther, the tiger, the leopard, which for the ancients were symbolic of the evil that looms over mankind: symbols of violence and destruction. The Bible, which mentions cats only once, in the Book of Baruch, puts them on the same footing as the two dark vices, treachery and lying. During the obscure, motley years of the Middle Ages, cats emerge surrounded by a malign, somber aura. Identified with the practices of witchcraft, they are thrown into the bonfires where their screams of pain blend with the cries of the women identified by the *vox populi* as guilty of sinful commerce with the devil. Cats and witches, objects of the same hunt, roasted by the same fires, fade away in unison before the exorcism of the flames. Cats, legend had it, sold their skins to the devil and on Saint John's Eve gathered at the witches' sabbath. Therefore they were condemned to perish in the flames on Easter Day, at the summer solstice, on Carnival Tuesday, or the first Sunday in

Lent. "The cat, who represents the devil, will never suffer enough." A basket full of cats, decorated with roses and garlands and set around with fireworks, was hoisted to the highest point in the crown of an enormous tree. Musicians and minstrels chanted joyful songs, and the authorities, sometimes the king himself, lit the sinister fire with torches of white and yellow wax. Freya, Nordic goddess of love and beauty, whose coach was pulled by two black cats, was long the object of orgiastic worship. The cats associated with her were believed not only to have a certain relationship with the devil but also with a debauched, sinful life. In Belgium during the first years of the 18th century, a royal decree prohibits the casting down of cats from the highest point of the cathedrals, a practice quite widespread in those days. But a hundred years later the prohibition is revoked. About that time, cats began to be accepted as company for human beings, although still only on unusual and exceptional occasions. More frequently they are exhibited as spectacles in cages at the fairs and in the first zoos. The timid beginnings of a fondness toward cats that suffered numerous ups and down in later years were manifest in the case of a Madamoiselle Dupuis who died about 1764 and left her cat the legacy of a lovely country house along with sufficient income to spend the rest of its days without privation.

The alleged cruelty of the cat is reflected, by a curious game of mirrors, in the cruelty of human beings who, by eliminating the cat, seek to free themselves, to exorcise something diabolic that they themselves bear within. Strange refractions of feelings between cat and man that during one epoch culminate tragically in the bonfire. Equally tragic but now in the domain of fantasy, cats are the key to a classic horror story by Edgar Allan Poe, "The Black Cat." Close and prolonged contact with a cat on the part of the story's main character awakens in him the malevolent instincts that induce him to destroy it. Another feline, a reincarnation of the one that was hanged, drives him to murder his wife. Nonetheless, the tale is ambiguous enough to suggest that this cat, the one which the narrator makes into the object of all his fears and hatreds, is actually his own conscience, the witness that is present at every moment to demonstrate to the man (who is inclined toward doing evil) his true image, without disguises. The cat is all tenderness, affection, loyalty. Its qualities are intolerable to its master, who must banish it from his sight in order to yield fully to his destructive impulses.

Through the cat, *Felix domesticus*, the threat of death is surreptitiously introduced into the vicinity of mankind, and it constitutes a pronounced reminder of how disintegration lies in wait for us. Beloved and feared, sought out and rejected, petted and tossed into the distance and oblivion, the cat's contradictory nature is the very reflection of human nature, of the urge to prevail, of the attraction (inexplicable but equally persistent) to what Thomas Mann calls "the abyss" and which the whole of Romantic literature values and elevates to the category of a cult: the inclination toward sickness and all its implications of disorder and death. It is no accident that Hoffmann, when he wants to transmit his most authentic message, attributes his reflections on life to Murr the cat. Pessimism, melancholy, an inclination toward the somber and the fantastic are the legacy of Romanticism. The cat has always inhabited the neighborhoods close to those worlds, redolent of exotic perfumes and dead bodies. It has flourished in rarefied atmospheres, in closed places, in the secret locales where all the flowers of evil germinate.

But even for Baudelaire, cats are at once the incarnation of good and evil. They are favored by both lovers and scholars who, "like them, are sedentary and sensitive to the cold. Friends of science and of voluptuousness, they seek out the silence and the horror of darkness." They would have been the mournful messengers of Erebus if it had been possible for them to bend their pride into service. "Great sphinxes sprawled in the depths of the lonely wastes, seeming to doze in an endless dream." Their eyes are golden and they enclose a mystical depth; a blend of metal and agate, profound and cold, they pierce like darts. Around cats there floats a subtle aura and a dangerous perfume. They are at once mysterious, seraphic, alien. Fairies or gods or messengers of death. When the poet wants to look into himself, to poke around within his spirit, he encounters an interior presence contemplating him with its pale pupils like living opals: this fixed gaze, that of a cat strolling around inside his brain as if in its own house, this is nothing other than the testimony of the spirit.

Privileged being, angel or demon, the cat represents a transcendent reality, beyond its physical nature and its animal condition: another world, a beyond, something that identifies it with the unknown. Since the first Biblical myth, any eagerness for knowledge is made worthy of punishment, and mankind, guilty of eating the forbidden fruit from the tree of the knowledge of good and evil, is condemned forever to an existence exiled from Paradise. Whenever the cat is identified with evil, it is because of its symbolic aspect as a link with the unknown. The presence of the cat, both static and extatic, its sovereign indifference, its voluptuous passivity, are masks disguising a peculiar tie. Just as the sphinx, which has so much of the feline animal about it, assures the perpetuation of some recondite millenary wisdom purloined from time and history; just as the oracle does not express the intentions of the being who merely lends it a voice but rather the designs of a deeper mystery, a destiny that escapes the will of human beings, so the cat shares in the condition of those intermediaries and is made worthy of the stigma accorded those who violate the sacred.

Before resorting to drugs, to hallucinogens and other stimuli capable of awakening sensibilities that have slept throughout many millenia of everyday activity, human beings under the influence of a nostalgia for the lost paradise, for a beginning where they might establish contact with the origins of life, with the ultimate *raison d'être*, find in the company of cats the certainty of a secret communication, the incentive, the suggestion, the fabulous illusion of a dimension that is meta-natural, meta-sensory, meta-physical. The cat that receives its caresses coolly and detached, as if it were present only in body, not in spirit, is a strange creature, a stranger in the sense Camus used it, a being come from very far off, from a place that one can only guess at and fear when it manifests itself through some exterior, concrete, visible sign such as the flight of certain birds, the appearance of some comet, or the somatic organization of a cat.

Cats also, therefore, are a little feminine, so much so that poets attribute to women an inaccessible, sibylline nature, a sixth sense that avoids structures erected with regard to logic, practical reason, and objective truth. In the affections of men, women share with cats an admiration that includes a certain terror, similar to the experience, often called religious, of remaining ignorant and defenseless in the face of events such as lightning, thunder, rain, or wind. Primitive man deifies the natural phenomena that amaze him and whose origin he does not know. Civilized man attributes to feline beings, women or cats, all those qualities that escape definition and have no regard for the rigorous inflexibility of anything that is reasonable, serious, and worthy of credit.

All superstitions exist at this level. In England, cats are often associated with ghosts, but even the very shape of a cat done in porcelain can bring on the greatest calamities, such as those suffered by the successive owners of the famous Chelsea Cat, a piece longed for by collectors but guilty of bringing down the wrath of fate upon those owners. In Kitchin's story the beautiful white porcelain cat transmits certain fateful, malign powers which came to it from its original: a cat of the same color, but one of flesh and blood, contemplating the tragic scene of the death of its owner's entire family, stricken by the plague around 1665. The image of this cat, created by an eccentric artist of Yorkshire named Samuel Hucks who accidently witnesses the family's agony and the relatively indifferent and perhaps satisfied air of the cat, is reproduced by an engraver, Amos Bolberry, who in turn dedicates the engraving, along with many others, to someone connected with the porcelain factory in Chelsea. There the figure is copied and the lovely white cat, turned into a work of art, embarks on its long career as a bearer of misfortune: it is known that one of its owners, Lord Innistarten, died of a shot to the head three days after having acquired it. Another died in an automobile accident after his wife had commited suicide and his three children had suffered many misfortunes. The next-to-last owner, a German prince, was stabbed to death in a concentration camp. Concerning the final owner, Lord Mallowbourne, the author of the story can only inform us (and he does this with a persistent British smile—and therefore an ironic, mocking one), that he is on the verge of going mad after his housekeeper falls ill with severe gall bladder pains and his cat Tompkins leaves the house one day, never to return. But the worst is when his personal physician smashes the malign porcelain cat to smithereens and then contracts a strange illness whose symptoms recall only too well those of the plague of 1665.

Nonetheless, not all Anglo-Saxon writers reveal their race's proverbial preference for dogs. Howard Phillips Lovecraft, originally from Rhode Island, visited infinite universes in his imagination without ever leaving the confines of New England, but among all the many living beings on earth he only bestowed his trust on the cat. In the mythical lands of demons and marvels travelled by Randolph Carter, the presence of cats is always beneficent and salving. Ulthar, the kingdom of the cats, is a gentle place, created to live in harmony until eternity. Muffled carillons of bells resound quietly from the church steeples, and that softness vibrates in the atmosphere of the city. But even there the cats slip along in secret toward those occult lands whose roads are known only to them, lands situated on the dark side of the moon toward which they gaze from the rooftops of the highest houses. In Ulthar the pillows are filled with perfumed herbs that induce sleep. An ancient law prohibits humans from killing cats, and the felines, taking over the city, stroll back and forth on the streets in graceful multitudes. In the temples of Ulthar the last copies of the Pnakotic manuscripts are kept, come down from time immemorial, written by men of the world of wakefulness, originally from forgotten kingdoms of the boreal regions. Those manuscripts contain revelations concerning the ancient gods, who used to dance by the light of the moon, and the city of the setting sun, the precinct of forgotten knowledge. Once more the presence of cats is associated with secret knowledge, the mysteries, the wisdom which entails some vague, obscure risk for humans. But in this case that knowledge is not related to the malign but to the beneficent; cats are the opposite of the abyss, and their beautiful, healthy forms rejoice the man who goes in search of the forgotten wisdom. In the enchanted forest, where the cats put his enemies to flight, they offer Carter their pleasant company, and after the victory they give themselves over to their fantastic capers or the nimble game of chasing dead leaves "that the wind caused to fly around among the mushrooms of that primitive ground."

In Lovecraft's fantasy universe, the demons are ghouls, bats, and other black animals of the night; among the marvels—actually in first place—are those lovely, kindly, perfect, privileged creatures, the cats. That extraordinary world through which Randolph Carter progresses, like Le Grand Meaulnes, is really the world of childhood illuminations, a miracle that is not to be found beyond the seas, nor on the mountain tops where the gods dance, but in the sun-drenched landscapes of New England, which are kept in the memory.

The cat, a symbol of all occult and mysterious wisdom, is also the emblem of freedom. In heraldry, this is what is symbolized when it elevates its rump higher than its head. The Romans had already noticed that characteristic, and Tiberius Graccus placed the effigy of a cat in the Temple of Freedom in Rome. This cat-like freedom is manifest in its sovereign independence with regard to human beings. The cat always keeps a part of its being veiled, and its friendship is not unconditional. Théophile Gautier warned us that this would never be offered us lightly, like that of the dog. The cat does not beg for our fellowship because it needs its own solitude and understands how to make use of it. If someone manages to pierce its wall of ancestral distrust and come close to a cat, the communication can become profound: a kind of silent inner dialogue that it is sometimes possible to sustain with very small children.

Cats, then, evoke worlds that belong not only to a beyond that is divine or satanic, or in other words, supernatural, but also to the lost paradise of childhood or the universe of absolute freedom where its being is sovereign and where it accepts no will other than its own. In the Romantic claptrap of castles, moonlit nights, ghosts and witches, the cat is a sign, a mark of the remotest past, of the days of gods, monsters, and mythical beings, the surviving witness of a consciousness dating back before that of humanity. Romantic literature, whether gloomy or gothic, is full of questions about the origin, the distance, the infinite antiquity contained within the cat's gaze. Later on, the cat is transformed from the symbol of a supernatural world situated outside humankind into a symbol of a beyond that is within us, in the depths of the soul. It becomes the suggestion of an interior world whose depths have no limit. To live in the shelter of that world has been our sin, on a par with the nature of intoxication, with transgression against an exterior order where any unusual conduct is condemned. We human beings have ended by putting ourselves on the same level as cats, by incorporating them into our being in order to turn them into the incarnation of a "descent into hell" at once both feared and desired, in that *déréglement de tous les sens* to which Rimbaud aspired and which now is sought for under other signs by introverts and the solitary multitudes, blending it with a mystical aspiration toward Love and the Absolute Good which claims to open wide the doors of perception.

In a story by Algernon Blackwood, "Ancient Sorceries," the supernatural as a remote past of witches' sabbaths and nameless gods coincides with the other world as something which always threatens human beings, attracting us with powerful spells. Something unnameable that draws the protagonist toward remote regions of time, regions "of fascinating beauty and terror," and at the same time something that also attracts him toward a dark, secret, internalized life that brings with it self-annihilation, the loss of one's being, the gentle, silent slide toward death. The character in "Ancient Sorceries" gets off a train by chance in a little village in the north of France. He wanders down narrow medieval alleyways and gradually begins to feel himself "comforted and stroked like a cat": "as if the warmth and stillness and the feeling of well-being would make me purr." At the inn, the corpulent owner seems like an enormous tabby cat, and at nightfall the town is like "a being lying there half asleep on the plain, purring." The inhabitants walk like cats, with muffled steps, and everything seems fluffy and velvety. The originally unintelligible warning offered by a travelling companion when he sees him getting off in that tiny station gradually acquires its full meaning: ... *à cause du sommeil et à cause des chats*, when Vezin feels himself more and more caught up in the invisible but palpable spider's web of that dark life drawing him subtly toward an ambiguous fusion with something impious, toward a feline second nature all the inhabitants of the town possess. This feline aspect is at once desireable and perilous because it assumes "a world so much larger and wilder than the one he had ever been accustomed to." In it a limitless, orgiastic freedom prevails, culminating in the Witches' Sabbath during which, women and men, transformed into elastic, sinuous cats are all overtaken by the frenzy of the dance. The sensuality, the eroticism, have something to do with death; they comprise, just as death does, a void in both body and spirit. The disintegration of death is contained within this erotic discourse.

As befits their strange nature, cats are of uncertain origin, which has disappeared without a trace in the millenia. All the links have been lost between the Miacis, a primitive creature which fifty million years ago used to wander over the plains and through the forests, and the saber-tooth tiger, which is the probable ancestor of the cat of our own times. It is just as if someone had erased the traces of the innumerable species that must have filled the prolonged space of time between the sabre-toothed tiger and the range of felids that nowadays inhabit the jungles of Central Asia, North Africa, and South America, the forests of Europe or the pampas of Argentina. Wildcats, leopards, linxes, mountain lions, cheetahs, pumas, all kinds of tigers. Was the Egyptian cat simply the ancient African wildcat, but domesticated? Where does the Siamese cat, known as the "cat of the temples," come from? Or the tailless cat native to the Isle of Man with no one knowing how it got there? And what names should we give our cats? Any name, whether reasonable or imaginative, will have the very defect that T.S. Eliot suggests: it will not express the ineffable, the inscrutable, the profound and the unique that humankind is incapable of discovering and that every living cat, submerged in deep meditation, is familiar with.

William Butler Yeats calls the cat "the closest relative to the moon," alluding to its nocturnal and slightly cold nature. Karel Capek assures us that it hears magical, mysterious voices when things begin to take on life in the midst of the darkness: the cat is an inhabitant of this darkness, the familiar of shadows, a perfect, sensitive soundbox capable of receiving signals invisible to other beings. Matthew Arnold guesses that it is a cruel but gentle being, filled with restraint, with a complexity of character that is given only to the most highly organized beings. Rudyard Kipling describes the cat as proud and solitary, incapable of servitude and sparing of friendship. Majestic and lordly, genteel and selective, is how Swinburne describes cats, while Colette, sheltered in cushy interiors and sharing with them their sophisticated refinement, intuits a superior nature in those ardent, fastidious, extremely sensitive creatures that seek euphoria by the light of a fire that she, who is so familiar with them, also knows how to share. Elective affinities have brought the secret worlds residing in the minds of cats together with individuals who perhaps have nothing else in common but that love of the vague territories of dreams: Samuel Johnson and Richelieu, Montaigne and Mallarmé, Edith Sitwell and the Baron de Montesquieu. For each of them, the company of cats has been a pleasure appropriate to unusual minds. Scarlatti dedicates a fugue to one of them, and Ravel calls them forth in *Les enfants et les sortiléges*, composed on a text by Colette. Their images, distant and majestic in Egyptian sculpture, fixed and hypnotic in the mosaics of Pompeii, undulating and a bit vampiresque in the Japanese drawings, turn classical in Pinturrichio, Barroccio, and Leonardo, and push aside the medieval and oriental other-worldliness; in Hogarth and the French painters of the eighteenth century, who bring them down to family scenes and surround them with children, as if to raise the curse that had weighed down upon them and restore them to the understandable proximity of human beings; and in the Romantic painters Géricault and Delacroix, with their love for the exotic and for all worlds present and suggested, the cats' halo of mystery and distance is returned to them.

Cats inhabit such splendid cities as Venice, which are also a little feminine, places where one lives in a world parallel to that of every day, but with a more intense reality of another order, like the reality of art. Venice, moreover, in its gilded Byzantine atmosphere, abode of memories and phantoms (Byron, and D'Annunzio, Wagner, Browning, and Henry James), shelters an incalculable number of cats, both live and carved in stone. As Mary MacCarthy said (her intuition concerning the city's cats coincides with that of the ancient books), the lions of Venice look like cats, or the cats, oddly enough, evoke the lions: the winged lion of San Marcos, transformed into a dragon, a basilisk, reproduced to infinity in the ancient dominions linked to the floating city, always so inclined to shipwreck, like a sumptuous, abandoned baroque vessel. And of course Paris loves its cats. The Paris of the "mysteries," the melancholy of the "children of the century," the elegies and night poems of Alfredo de Musset.

Cats reside in all those lands where reality is not limited to itself but is surrounded by an aura, a trembling: that kind of levitation which sustains things within some paintings whose backgounds are constituted by something dense that gives off the vibrancy of life and communicates it to objects; those dwellings of the spirit where, as Leopardi would have wished, love and death become joined together; those "spaces of another life" where human beings are transported by the torments of the soul, according to Chateaubriand; all the places anywhere in the world where the ardent heroes of Romanticism long to find some refuge forever exiled from the everyday, from bourgeois banality. If Goethe's definition were still valid and we were to label "Classical" anything that is healthy and "Romantic" anything sick, it would be easy without hesitation to identify cats with those somber, twilight states of being that people who consider themselves healthy attribute, naturally, to illness. But we would be simplifying too much. Because if it is true that human beings have attributed to cats those qualities in themselves that associated them with the shadows, they have also attributed to them the most lucid tendencies and most creative forces of their being—perhaps through an obscure intuition that beauty, which is in itself indefinable, always assumes a certain structure, a certain organization, a certain order; and that wherever the harmony of form surges up like a miracle in the midst of what used to be falling apart, one is sure that there has also been something equally indefinable, a force sufficiently integrative to introduce order and life into the company of chaos and death. The cat, the mirror in which human beings have projected their own image as if through infinite prisms, collects all the dispersed facts, reconstitutes them, and returns us to the security of a lengthy survival, having been given prestige by that intact, hallmark beauty which belongs to it.

At least, that is the illusion we humans have. Because every cat, the repository of a wisdom that is not given to us to achieve, shares the property Lewis Carroll granted the Cheshire Cat of being able to disappear gradually until nothing but its smile is left. An ironic smile that keeps us and will always keep us at a prudent distance and will not allow us to forget the immensity of our smallness nor the immoderacy of our arrogance.

I

Celina
or the
Cats

Celina and I were married for thirteen years. It's not that I believe in superstitions. I know the number thirteen is a number just like any other number. There is even something oddly attractive about it. But the fact is that our marriage lasted for thirteen years, and that suffices to make me unable to avoid giving this number some cabbalistic significance or envisioning it whenever I think of it (or think of Celina) as surrounded by something somber and, I might even say, almost mysterious or hallucinatory. Nevertheless it is not a question of anything concrete. Or rather I would have to explain how at the beginning of that thirteenth year of our union (I say "that year" because it has already passed, because today is the day after yesterday, which was the last day of our thirteen years; today is the first day on which we are no longer married, on which I am alone again) everything that had happened in the previous twelve years began to find a place in a different order which only then took shape, a totality which for me had the finished and certain aspect of something that already existed, something that had matured, that would culminate in a moment which could not last beyond that year and which would then disappear completely. Now that I see it all from here, from this day when I have set myself to writing about what has occurred because I cannot do anything else, it seems to me that everything was very clear from the beginning (the beginning of that year) and that from the moment I am referring to but which I would not be able to determine more precisely, I knew exactly and assuredly what was going to happen, how and when it was to happen.

I don't know where to start. Neither do I know if I was to blame. The strange thing is that at the time when I first began to be more clearly conscious of the things that might happen (and that were actually taking place), I also began to lose all notion of good and evil and, above all, of my responsibility in the course of events. I ceased to be aware of that odd sensation of heaviness and detachment that had first begun to materialize only gradually. Celina and I and the cats began to be like tokens in some inexorable game being manipulated by a diabolic player who, I am almost certain, might well be the devil himself. As I go back just now and reread what I have written it seems rather odd to me. I mean it is not anything I would normally have thought. Because I must confess that I have not believed in God for a long time nor, until now—whenever "now" began—in the devil, either. And I should also mention that I have always been a practical and what is usually called a successful man.

I am a physician. To be more precise, a famous physician, a well-known, very competent surgeon. Until yesterday, at least. And if it were not for the fact that now a number of things have ceased to be important to me, it would surely be gratifying to imagine that what has happened might manage to surround me with a kind of spectacular prestige, or to describe it more clearly, it might add to the seductiveness possessed by some individuals (with regard to women, of course) that is not easy to pin down but that forms a part of certain obscure, ambiguous situations.

By the time I married Celina I had made a small fortune. My father was an unassuming lawyer and he left me neither very much money nor too many contacts. But I have always had not only an innate talent for awakening the confidence of others, but also the sort of charm which is extremely helpful in a profession such as mine. Besides, I possess an unusual intuition for diagnosis in addition to these hands, so subtle and steady that they used to be the envy of all my colleagues. Truly, I have a surgeon's hands. I liked to think that I had been born predisposed to devote my life to saving the lives of others. I can swear that I never thought of anything else nor was I ever seduced by the idea of injuring anyone, of doing anyone harm, or of being unfaithful to the oath I keep in my office and that I have never failed to read every single day of my professional life. I say this not so much to justify myself but because it is the truth and because I cannot help having some regard for the inexplicable contrast between those personality traits and that other part of myself that I never had known about, that began to manifest itself after several years of marriage, and that I can only explain through Celina, in the degree that we began to seem so like one another.

I met Celina at a party. I was just starting my career then, and despite the fact that I was working hard at the hospital, in my office, visiting my patients, I always took the time to attend those social get-togethers because they seemed very useful for extending my practice. My mother's family afforded me certain convenient contacts and access to elegant circles. That atmosphere had, moreover, exercised a strange seductiveness. The first invitations opened many doors for me and very quickly I became one of the dependable ones. Little by little, the more broadly my reputation as a good internist and better surgeon spread, the more exclusive and less numerous were the circles I got into; but by then I could allow myself that luxury because my clientele was already established. I am not certain, but it seems to me that there was a kind of voluptuousness among the motives of those who turned me into a habitué of their gatherings. A voluptuousness that consisted in making me a participant in those bursts of frivolity and unconcern—I who had just removed a small tumor from some delicate organ or who was more aware than anyone of an incipient pulmonary weakness or who recognized the more or less advanced symptoms of one of those transitory diseases that are not usually talked about. But I should recognize that I was a long way from perceiving this at the time, and I allowed myself to become infected in the most ingenuous and enthusiastic way with the happy sounds of the noisy music and the vertigo of the dancing that would start up midway through the party, or even later, so that I often had to interrupt it because of the inopportune call of some apprehensive patient.

From where I am at this moment, in this sixth floor apartment with a view of the ocean (it is located at a corner; the ocean is scarcely two blocks away, and between my building and the ocean there is no other high edifice) as well as of the avenue which I like so much with its double row of palm trees down the center, everything I am telling about seems very far away and rather outside me, as if I were speaking with someone about things that had been happening to a mutual acquaintance. In reality, everything did happen to a person who I no longer am, although for those who knew me back then I continue being the same as before, the same as always, the ingenuous but self-seeking young man turned into a solid physician one could always depend on, in whom one could always confide. And now, when the news gets around, they will think of me with compassion, with sympathy, as if I had nothing to do with what has occurred, as if, in a word, I were the true victim. There is a portion of this whole affair that would support that judgment. But there is also the other part. Because how can I deny that at a certain moment I stopped being a victim and turned into a party to the crime and therefore, in a strange way, into a murderer?

I don't know why it seems impossible for me to tell what I should without continually falling into these digressions. Perhaps it is because this is the first time that I am able to see it all from the outside, since after all, what happened yesterday has freed me from something and I need to find in it an order to all this disorder, to put words, many words, between what I might be today—now—and incoherence.

I have lived here for some time. For three years. Maybe four. I've been living here since Celina and I separated. It was then that I began to occupy once and for all this space that I had previously used as a study to get away for a while when Celina would have the house full of people whom I knew less and less and when I was starting to prefer the solitude. Later on I used this place to put the greater part of the city between her bedroom, always drowsing in the strange greenish half-light that the curtains made when the sun shone through them as she slept, and the place—any place—where I was.

I could swear it was not I who sought the separation. I loved Celina; that is the truth. When I met her, she was very young. Probably no older than sixteen.

I never did know what color her eyes were. Why do I think now about the color of Celina's eyes? It was an indefinite color, one that changed a great deal with the light. But I would be unable to fix with certainty on any definite shade between green and chestnut brown. No doubt there was some yellow pigment there which would mingle with two or three other colors within that range so that a shine would prevail, similar to that of some bodies that only reflect light yet seem to be giving off their own. Not always, of course. But later on I realized that she knew how to place herself in such a way that the ambient light would favor this impression. I was never able to confirm it, but I know that she had spent many hours studying this with a mirror placed before her, in a state of morbid curiosity about herself that made her take delight in scrutinizing the texture of a small fragment of her skin, the tiniest hairs that sprang from her fingers, the wrinkle-like lines that crossed the back of her hand, her fingernails, her hands. Celina loved her own hands.

I often used to say to her, with a pretentiousness that surely made her smile inside (I always had the impression that she was laughing to herself in this fashion without anything giving her away except a slightly different shine to her eyes), I would say that if I had been a painter I would have done a portrait of her in which her two clasped hands would stand out with an almost violent light. Because I too adored Celina's hands, and I think it was impossible to be with her without immediately fixing on them. Celina never painted her nails but she would work on them with near fanatic dedication, for which she had a *polissoir* and a very complete arsenal of little scissors and tweezers. I would also tell her, joking, that they looked like a miniature set of surgeon's instruments. With a white pencil she would accent the color on the underside of the outer part of the nail, and after she had finished the lengthy, daily operation, she applied a transparent polish that brought out the natural tones. I might say that her hands were quite long, with her fingers extended in a gentle, perfect oval, or that those hands had something aristocratic and distant about them, as if they had never been made to be touched nor to caress anything, but only to greet the multitudes from a distance, from inaccessible balconies or from open, unapproachable automobiles— but to say all this has nothing to do with the essential aspect of Celina's hands.

I wonder, in the situation where I find myself, why it has occurred to me for the first time to attempt to set a framework of words around the things that have happened, and

I think that as I write about them those things are beginning to mean something for the first time. A moment ago I brought up two words with regard to all this—disorder, incoherence. Now I would like to add another: disintegration. Something that used to be very clear, quite luminous, has fallen apart. And I feel an uncontrollable impulse obliging me to contain this dispersal, to fix it—and perhaps to fool myself into thinking it will be fixed forever.

I did not feel the need to sleep last night. After returning here I sat myself down in an easy chair in front of the window and smoked a pack and a half of cigarettes. But at a certain point, approximately three quarters of an hour ago (that is, about an hour and a half after dawn had commenced), I got up from that chair, came over to sit down at the desk, picked up a pen and several sheets of paper that have always been here because this is not where I have my office and so I have never needed them for anything else, and started to write this account as if I suddenly wished to exhaust with a single stroke all of the lucidity accumulated over a lengthy period.

The strange thing is that I have not felt any horror. I've not felt any remorse, either. What has happened has only been the natural culmination of a process that bore this end within itself; nothing and no one could have altered it.

That day when I saw her for the first time, Celina was dressed in lilac. Later I found out that this was her favorite color and that everything she wore had at least a tiny bit of lilac in it, in different hues and intensities from rosewood to violet. During the first year of our marriage I had her portrait done wearing that dress, and this is the one I brought here to my study when I moved in for good. Now my back is turned to it as I write, but I do not need to look at it since I know it so well, I would say millimeter by millimeter. The artist, one of those academic painters that come into vogue, did not do what I would have done, that is, he did not accentuate her hands, but surprisingly he still managed to give the portrait a singular glow, something which I perceived the very first time I saw it. This glow radiates from Celina's eyes and draws one in toward a greater depth, a further level, an inwardness that is not disturbing but something fresh, tenuous, placid. That's the way she was in those days. Was she really? Of course. She was like that all the time we lived in our first apartment, two blocks from here (this is strange! I hadn't realized it until just now!), when we saw almost no one, she would wait for me at night, always awake, and we loved each other in an elemental, passionate way.

I was obsessed with having her portrait done. Every year it was a different painter, a different dress, a different background. But it turned out to be quite futile. Celina gradually absented herself from her portraits more and more, and in the two last ones, what I would call the soul of Celina had disappeared completely. That was during the sixth year. It was just as though Celina had died.

I wondered greatly in those days how this could have come to pass. It was a slow but inevitable process. At first Celina was cheerful, with a joyousness that did not recognize its own negation, that was complete in itself and did not need the premonition of its possible absence in order to prevail. Never have I seen anyone be happy in the same way Celina was. Whatever state she was in, she was so in exactly the same way—with an intensity that was exhausting, thorough, implacable. (This very moment I have the feeling I want to embrace her.) And each time, to be as she was at that moment, which might last months or years, or perhaps scarcely a few weeks, was her only purpose, one she adhered to fiercely, from something rooted deeply within her like a rock, something hard and perfect. Hard and perfect. Maybe that is what Celina was—something hard and perfect. And how could something like that just disappear?

One night we were returning from a party. Celina had given me the impression all evening of being radiant, engulfed in a state of euphoria that was no surprise to me because that was her state of mind at the time and I was sure that this impression of overflowing high spirits was going to last forever. I was humming a tune as we entered the apartment. I left the keys on the dresser, took off my coat, and casually went into the bathroom as if I were alone, so confident was I of that unshakable harmony we had between us. When I returned to the living room, probably while taking off my tie (I know these details are not important, and moreover it is impossible to recall them after all the time that has passed, but I feel, and I do not know why, that it is necessary to reestablish something by means of setting the smallest, most insignificant incidents in their due place, with the least margin of equivocation), all right then, I repeat, when I came back into the living room loosening the knot of my tie, I sat down facing Celina and lazily stretched my legs.

"Why did you leave me alone? I was afraid."

"Afraid? Of what?"

"I don't know. I don't know exactly. Suddenly I felt like something was going to happen to me. How could you leave me alone?"

She looked at me strangely, as if that very strangeness were much better defined than the fear she said she had felt just a moment ago.

"I was afraid I was going to die."

I tried to take it as a joke. Die? At her age? (To me, Celina continued to be just a little girl.) How could such a thing occur to her? Didn't she want for us to have a little drink? The last one? We would go to bed, and then, I hinted, I would make love to her and her fears would pass.

Celina barely smiled. Men, she told me insinuatingly, always think they can resolve everything with that. For the first time, I felt lost facing Celina. (Later on, feeling myself lost began to be a normal situation.) Celina looked at me and— strange how one so unexpectedly discovers the most obvious things—then I realized I was seated in an easy chair smoking a cigarette. Because to hide my discomfort as we were talking I had taken one out of the silver cigarette case a patient had given me and that I liked very much and that was always beside my favorite chair. And it is here now, beside the same chair, tempting me to sit myself down in the same spot and start smoking. But what is going on here? Why this incapacity to concentrate, to stick to the course of events? The facts seem to be escaping my grasp, coming undone. They are being eroded, and I need to find support in the gestures, in this or that little word recollected, in the memory of those things that surrounded me, in order to shore up my memory of what was happening. Because I am on the verge of believing that nothing happened at all and that if I were to get up from here right now and go down the stairs, get in my car, and drive to Celina's house, I would find her as always at this hour, asleep in her securely closed room, guarded by the cats.

To return to that moment, I realized that I, who was seated in an easy chair smoking, was a person, I had a given name, Carlos Manuel, and a family name, and that this person that I am was completely cut off from that other person who was Celina.

And I felt relieved. The worst thing was that I felt relieved. And with a lucidity that one only acquires by accident, as if a spirit were visiting one (I myself am surprised by expressions like this, but I cannot avoid them), I understood that Celina had felt precisely the same thing, except that for her this sensation had not been a relief but the fear that had made her suddenly believe herself to be endangered by death.

"Why don't you love me the way I do you? Why do you resist? I need you so much. There's so little time! If you were to leave me . . ."

That night was when our trials began. Celina needed me. But she needed me as a part of her. She had to incorporate me into herself as if I were one of her hands or a lung. She needed me in order to breathe, to live. Celina needed me as an intermediary. Someone who would allow her to relate to the world without exposing herself too much. At first I let myself become involved. It was a fascinating game. Moreover, it flattered me. I cannot deny that it gave me pleasure to allow her to do this and to lend myself to her, to permit her to make use of what I did in order to compensate for her own inactivity, to let her manage my time and my activities as if they were her own. This came to be as indispensable to me as it was to her, and when I went off in my car to visit my patients or when I entered the operating room, it seemed to me as though Celina was accompanying me, that I had not been separated from her; it seemed as though she had assimilated so many of my idiosyncracies that she now really formed part of me. Because Celina did not force me to devote my time exclusively to her, taking it out of my working hours; she fixed things so as to be a part of that time at every moment. She participated so thoroughly in my cases, in my patients' histories, that she knew as much as I did, and she was so fully involved in the way I spent my time that in the most literal way she shared what my life was like outside the house.

It was a kind of intoxication. The moment arrived when I could not do without it. It wasn't she but I who called up on the telephone every little while in order to confirm that she was at home waiting for me. I preferred that she not go out, that she devote her time to nothing else, that she be interested in nothing but me, that she not even read the newspapers.

Secretly, I was enjoying Celina's idleness. But then she started to manage her fantasies. She wanted to intervene more directly, to force me to reduce the time I spent with

patients who displeased her, to make me miss certain appoint-
ments, or to reject a case that promised to be interesting. She
did all this innocently but with the same decisiveness she
applied to anything where she focussed her will. Because that
was Celina's strength—the passion with which she was able to
defend her weakness. That was her hardness. And her perfection. And when that intensity, that hardness, and that perfection
apparently vanished, she went in the opposite direction, turning herself pitilessly inward toward her own self. For in all that
came later, this was her only aim.

It would be very difficult for me to put everything from
that time in order. I must resign myself to these fragments.
There was something dizzying about those things, and moreover, time seemed totally free, infinitely open to our whims.

I really liked the apartment we had then. It was simple,
with little furniture, but everything in good taste. There were
the indispensable things in every corner, a table with a lamp,
a wide, comfortable chair. Not too much of anything. It was a
luxurious place, with a marble floor and huge windows opening out toward the ocean, but everything was sober and seemed
to fulfill a function. The curtains were clear and transparent, to
allow light in and awaken me early.

How different this place was from the home we bought
later on! Or rather, that Celina bought, with her own money, as
though she wanted to shut me out.

Because by that time, when we moved, Celina had
already begun to draw away from me. It is true that as I was
getting more and more interested in my career, this sort of
double self, or shadow, that was Celina had begun to weigh on
me. But I allowed things to take their course. I would never
have forced them. I never said anything to her. Perhaps it was
simply that there was something in my way of talking to her,
something too cautious, that sought to hide a more profound
desire to keep myself at a distance, on the margin, safe and

sound. People often say, it's almost a commonplace, that after many years of marriage, couples end by physically resembling each other. I always used to laugh at that. I didn't believe in it. It was just one of the banalities that everyone repeats over and over again through inertia and sometimes with some satisfaction, even though they know it doesn't mean anything. And suddenly people who weren't acquainted with us were asking if we were brother and sister; or, if we had just been introduced, they would wonder aloud, with an amused and slightly malicious air, how was it possible, how could we be man and wife, we must love each other a great deal, and other things like that. It wasn't the details of our clothing, it wasn't our features. It was a reciprocal assimilation by one of us of the other. And the strange thing is that it was I who was reproducing—without intending to, of course—the tone, the smile, the very words Celina used. As for me, when I realized it, it was to confirm a softening of my personality, or to tell it as I saw it then, a feminization. I would look at myself in the mirror trying to catch a shine in my eyes similar to the shine Celina had in hers, trying to surprise in the way I close my lips the frown produced in the corners of Celina's mouth, which were slanted upward naturally without the aid of lipstick. And I would laugh, laughing only in front of the mirror; or I would open my eyes in surprise, or pretend displeasure, doing all this as I assumed Celina did it in order to see how much, to what extreme we resembled each other. This all seems ridiculous to me now. But then it was an obsession which never left me in peace. I had to avoid her, to see her less, to make her go alone to those places where I always used to go, and I had to do it without her realizing it, without arousing any suspicion. (I should add that in everything Celina continued to display an elemental innocence, an ingenuous openness that was not feigned but which was a part of her, an ignorance of anything suspect or even dreadful in her conduct, as happens with some cruel children.)

In those days I would come home furtively, when I thought she would not be at home; I contrived the impossible to eat out, and I piled on some more or less professional obligations after my office hours in order to arrive home after midnight, fearing and at the same time hoping to encounter her reproaches, her wrath. But futilely, because Celina never reproached me for anything, she never asked me anything, she behaved as though nothing mattered to her, as though I myself were concerning her less all the time. It has been raining for a while now. I had not realized it. I just went over to look out the window. It is raining fairly hard, and it is really strange that I would not have heard the rain until now. The sky is very low; it is that color of gray that seems blue. There is thunder. This must have been the first time because I would not have been able to keep from hearing so loud a racket. I had turned on the light after it began to get dark without thinking that when it gets dark this way it is because it is going to rain. Then suddenly the lights went out. That is why I went over to the window. I have just looked at the clock, and it is three in the afternoon. Three o'clock! How many hours have gone by! I have not eaten anything. I'm not hungry. There are almost no cigarettes left.

The lights are back on. If not, with this afternoon shut down so, I could not write, I would not be able to see what I am writing. There are times when the light takes so long to . . . Once it happened to me when I was operating, and the hospital had no backup power. That was a bad time. It seems to me that I am seeing Celina as she was that afternoon.

The truth is that I suffered from many delusions. We had been in the new place for a month when she wanted to give a big housewarming party. She invited scores of people. She even had an orchestra brought in. I did not take part in any of the preparations. We had not seen each other the whole day. It was still light out when I arrived at seven, on one of those long summer days when the moon comes out around six or seven in a clear sky and by eight o'clock the sky still has not changed its color. It was quite breezy. An evening made for such a party—that is what it seemed like. I recall that, opening the door, I wondered what would happen if I had been mistaken, if this were the wrong day, if there would be no flowers when I came in, nor sounds of silverware and dishes, nor conversations of a slightly scandalous air in the kitchen. I would open the door, and Celina would be descending the stairs, dressed in lilac with her hair falling in a heavy wave over her left cheek. I would see her once more as I had the first time. Nothing would have changed. She would kiss me but say very little. She would take me by the hand through the whole house, she would show me the table, make me go into the kitchen, make me hurry upstairs to change. She would say to me, "It's so nice of you to get here in time. You're not going to come home late any more, are you?"

The lights were already on when I came in, although outside the darkness had not arrived as yet. I don't think I had noticed until then that the house was indeed sumptuous. At that moment I felt gratified, almost as if I had chosen it and purchased it to give to Celina, wrapped in cellophane.

She was coming out of her room as I started up the stairs. She wasn't wearing lilac but a dress in that raw color of Chinese silk; I think her dress was actually made of this material. She wasn't even wearing a pearl necklace. But her hair, yes, it was just as I had imagined. I had never seen her look so dazzling.

When we met on the stairs she said, "What a surprise! Aren't you keeping your office hours today?"

She continued going down with such rapidity that she gave me no time to answer her. I then started up the stairs very slowly, wishing they would never end. She had left the whole way impregnated with her perfume. Never have I noticed this perfume on any other woman. Yesterday I recognized it again when I entered her bedroom after so long a time. Once, in a fashion magazine I came across somewhere, I saw the name of Celina's perfume together with a slogan that I read several times so as not to forget the words: "Cyprus, a feminine perfume par excellence, is extracted from oak moss, a species of lichen." But it wasn't the perfume, that was not it. I needed to give myself time to recall Celina's words in some other fashion, to give them a tone less aggressively indifferent, to place them on the same level, almost, with the words I had imagined. By the time I finished dressing I had practically succeeded in doing this. The idea that they might ruin my whole evening was something I would not accept. I went down and greeted the first guests, feeling confident and assured, capable of allowing myself unlimited stimulation by the alcohol, the conversation, the women.

I moved around at random, always glass in hand, without settling anywhere, talking with friends, exchanging pleasantries with the ladies, but not wanting to remain very long in any one spot. I went out on the terrace. Nighttime had fully arrived. Some couples were strolling through the park in front of me, and the air was extremely pleasant. A ship was entering the bay. I could not distinguish the people on deck, leaning against the railing, because the ship was so extravagantly lit up and the lights' glare erased everything else. The image of a ship heavy with lights was frequent at this hour, but that day, what with the drinks, the sounds of the people, and the feeling of irresponsibility the party had given me, something surged up from within me stronger than at other times; it was the same idea suggested to me as a child by similar boats, and that was the desire to go away some place—any place, and I do not know why I always thought of British Columbia—the desire to be an eternal passenger on one of those luminous, white ships. A young woman drew me back inside to dance.

After that I didn't stop the whole night long. I was a whirlwind. I do not recall who I was with, but I know that I danced until the end, and not once with Celina. Neither did I search her out. I noticed her from a distance, dancing with others, and it gratified me to harbor the idea that, although everyone else might desire her, I was the only one who would be able to make love to her when the house was quiet after the party.

I think people began to leave at about two in the morning. At the end there were only a few of the more intimate friends left. I went up to my room and did not come back down again, with the result that even they were gone in about half an hour, despite Celina's resistance, for she tried to hold them back. I put on my pajamas and bathrobe in a leisurely way and went into her room. She, on the contrary, had changed rapidly and was already lying down with the light out. I lay down beside her, caressed her neck, and waited. She did not move. But I was determined. I came closer and kissed her at length on the shoulder. Without moving, Celina allowed me to touch her as if she were somewhere else. After a while she responded suddenly with a violence that for a moment I mistook for rising passion, only to realize that this was a way of rejection and aggression. I lit a cigarette and was intending to finish smoking it before going back to my room, when Celina spoke, as though from the first moment she had been preparing what she was going to say to me:

"I don't know how I could have . . . At any rate, it will be for the last time."

"The last time? What's the matter with you, why do you say that? The last time for what?"

"I can't bear it any longer. You don't love me. And besides— But that doesn't matter now. It just irritates me. You irritate me. I want to be alone. Go away."

I went back to my room and slept soundly until nearly noon. The heaviness caused by the alcohol did not let me spend a lot of time over what Celina had said, nor could I, for the same reason, give it too much importance even though I might have wanted to. She had gone out by the time I got up. I had nothing to do that morning, but after bathing and dressing I went to the office. Then it occurred to me that I needed a place for myself, for when I was not at home. But I did nothing yet. I had almost forgotten the business with Celina—well, no, actually I did remember, but it seemed to me that she had said those things a long time ago and that as soon as I saw her again she would speak to me in her normal way, with the coolness that was now her habit but nothing more, just like every day.

I returned home very late, and Celina had not come back. I left the door open to my room in order to hear her when she arrived, but I must have fallen asleep immediately because I never knew what time she came in.

The following day we met at the breakfast table, and Celina treated me just as I had imagined. Nothing had happened. My God! How could have I known Celina so imperfectly?

That party was the first. Later there came others. Celina gave one every two weeks, then every week, until there were people in the house two or three times a week. I don't know if the guests were always the same ones. That was hardly the most important thing. It was simply that Celina could not be by herself; she needed the commotion, and her friends were with her every day until rather late; and when there was nothing doing at home she always had something to do away from it. After the first few times, I did not return to the parties. It was then that I started to look for this apartment where I could be alone, and I sought always to arrange for some unavoidable commitments so it wouldn't be necessary for me to be present at all. Anyone would have said I was seeking excuses to feel jealous of Celina. Possibly so. The truth is that it soon began to be an obsession for me to wonder if Celina had a lover. I didn't seek her out at all because I still seemed to be hearing her words that night, and she, the few times we saw each other, acted as though this strange way of living were the most natural in the world. She would speak to me from time to time, about her parties, about some of her guests, about how much fun she was having—this always in the mornings over breakfast—but she never asked me why I never attended. The possibility that Celina might have a lover was fading away. Occasionally I would have little adventures, but they never lasted for long. I got accustomed to the changes in our relationship, and I came to think that eventually the same thing happens to all marriages, that they all have to go through different phases of closeness and separation (I scarcely thought any more about my alleged resemblance to Celina), and that things would go on this way indefinitely, thus giving our marriage a certain stability even though it was based, paradoxically, on our progressive estrangement.

All this lasted for some months, not many, but I really do not know how long it was. Until one day the parties ended, just like that. For a long time still, the phone would ring insistently. The most assiduous party-goers kept calling Celina, finding it strange not to be receiving any invitations. Then, little by little, they tired of this and went away. I know this because during that period I contrived to spend long periods at home, as if I were expecting something to happen, even though I spent those periods alone in my room, with Celina alone in hers. One day when I was asleep during the siesta, some irritating noises which at first I could not identify awakened me. Then I realized that someone was moving furniture around from one place to another, that someone was repeatedly going up and down the stairs.

When I went into Celina's room, everything was in confusion: clothing on the floor or draped over the chairs, shoes on top of the cabinets, and all the new furniture still haphazardly set down away from the walls and not yet moved to their destined places. There was much more than would normally have been able to fit into that room, I told myself. Even I, who knows nothing about styles, was able to distinguish that this was in the vein of Empire. Then I saw Lydia for the first time.

Lydia moved about among all that disorder as if she were capable of setting things right in a trice, imposing an order on it which just as quickly acquired a definitive stamp. This impression that she gave me then, that she has always given me, has to do with her way of walking exceptionally straight, with her impeccable white uniform, her thick, neutrally colored stockings that cover her legs completely, her sturdy shoes with military heels, her hair pulled back into a very small bun behind her head, but above all with her dominating gestures and the sharp accent of her badly pronounced Spanish which she made no effort to speak well—all of which emanate from her as the outer signs of an institution that is unshakable, one that she faithfully represents. Strangely, that vocation of Lydia's for an apparent kind of order served to give support to or perhaps even to favor the indisputable implantation of an element of decadence in Celina's ever more closed world.

When Celina saw me, she merely inclined her head in the servant's direction, and said, "This is Lydia."

And immediately she followed up, condescendingly, "Lydia took care of me when I was little. She has been in Jamaica seeing her family. Now she will never leave me again. Isn't that right, Lydia?"

The woman didn't answer. She looked at Celina as if my wife were her little cub and I, the intruder, were about to snatch her away. Her expression showed tenderness, of course, but also something terribly possessive and dominating. I recall how it irritated me to find her using the familar *tú* with Celina and how impotent I felt about making her change her manner of speech.

Celina asked me if I liked her new furniture. I told her I did, but at bottom I felt it produced a peculiar discomfort in me that I would not have known how to put into words, although I understood it better a few days later when I entered the room again under the pretext of searching for a tie pin I had lost. I had had it in my hand, I explained with childish awkwardness, when the room was all turned upside down because of the changeover.

A huge black carpet with garlands of enormous flowers, red roses, and green foliage, and a white fringe all around, covered nearly the whole floor. Despite the fact that the exquisite, pearl-colored *chaise-longue* placed in front of the window made me think of the famous portrait of Madame Recamier, and I could imagine Celina reclining there with a tunic and an indifferent smile, perhaps disguised as Pauline Bonaparte, I did not feel like laughing. It would not be exaggerating were I to say that it gave me the shivers. I had the impression of contemplating the performance of a play that was sophisticated, unpleasant, but nevertheless tragic.

The image I have of that room is the one from that day. As though I had photographed it with a part of my memory where only certain things are kept, very special things that I would doubtless need some day.

I am sure that the same furniture in some other place would have had a very different effect on me. Not all of it was the same color, but a dark honey tone was predominant. There was a very restrained desk with long, thin legs and a single, long drawer, very thin, with drawer pulls in the form of laurel crowns. There were small chests with marble tops—white, black, and rose-colored marble with white veins—with gilded edges and little winged sphinxes on the legs; there were also rounded chairs with feet like claws. The bed was quite similar to the *chaise-longue* by the window, with a dark canopy the same color as the draperies. The window also had white curtains, but that day (and I believe it was always so), the heavy green draperies were almost closed over the curtains, and the sunlight, no matter how strong, was changed into a greenish half-light that gradually turned somber as the day passed and evening came on.

I have the impression of having seen a similar room, furnished just like Celina's but somewhere else, but with a freshness and clarity that was never seen in Celina's bedroom again once the furniture was put in. I don't know. Probably not. I think I only saw it in my imagination the first time I entered the room and encountered this peculiar light which I recall, as if it summed up everything else, with bothersome fidelity and a persistence that has followed me ever since. And this in spite of my desire to leave it all behind, to forget that sickly, funereal light, the odor of confinement that very soon became mixed with the cats' odor, the figure of Celina always reclining on her bed as if she were sick, the exaggerated cleanliness that was there at first, and the filth that gradually was introduced later on when Celina managed partly through pleading and partly through insistence to get Lydia to stop cleaning every day in order to keep the dust from giving her asthma—though I am certain that she never suffered from any complaint of that sort during the time I knew her. My desire to forget all this—I have not been able to satisfy it even now. Nor my desire to dismiss from my mind, during all that followed, the Chinese screen that looked so absurd alongside the furniture, the ivory figures her father gave her when she was a little girl, the three seashells with pearls inside, all imbedded in a glass block. And that enormous painting, so strident, so out of place that it always seemed about to jump off the wall and fall down on you, done by a Spanish painter named Romero de Torres, which she had also inherited, showing three women wearing mantillas leaning out of a box overlooking a bull fight.

I have just poked my head out the window again. It keeps raining. And by now it is completely dark. Twenty-four hours have gone by. There is some wind. Down where the automobile lights are, the rain is being pulled sidewise.

I want to forget, and nonetheless I cannot think about anything else. Perhaps when I have finished writing everything . . .

At first Celina continued going out, though always very late in the day, at a quarter to six in the afternoon, for example, to stop in at some shop, when she knew perfectly well that all the stores closed at six. Lydia would accompany her. Later on she ended by giving up those futile sorties (I say "futile" because they never served the purpose for which they were intended) and shut herself up in her room with no attempt now to dissimulate. Sometimes, but less and less, a friend would come by to see her during the afternoon, when Celina had just started eating (she would wake up between twelve and one to have breakfast), and Lydia would come in with another tray bearing a snack for the visitor. Although from time to time I used to be in my room at that hour, I never heard what Celina talked about with her friends because the door to the bathroom that lay between our bedrooms was never open.

I don't know how Celina managed to get the cats. Perhaps they were Lydia's idea, or else that of some of the friends who still used to see her, as a way of providing Celina some entertainment. Maybe they brought her one or two and then she became attached to them. It could be that she had Lydia look for ads in the newspaper, or maybe she herself put one in soliciting cats with such and such characteristics. I assume all this, but I do not know for certain. I only know that she had never had any pets in the time I had known her, nor had she shown interest in or special attraction to them. Nevertheless, she eventually had nearly a dozen cats in her room.

There were angora cats, Persians, Siamese; I can't be

absolutely certain, but there is no doubt that they were extremely elegant cats. Grays and whites, and one completely honey-colored cat, similar to the color of the furniture, though slightly paler. (I notice that I said "were," as if with this word I would be able to erase them completely from the world, as from my memory. But are words enough?)

The cats lived on the chairs, the carpet, Celina's bed. Lydia shooed them off at certain hours, I saw her do it several times, but anyone who stopped in the doorway (I do not think I ever actually went inside the room again) had to make an effort not to swallow the unavoidable odor of the cats along with one's breath. And in spite of everything I was unable to put a stop to my habit of pausing at her door every afternoon. This was the only time now, day or night, that I saw Celina. I asked her how she was feeling, if she needed anything, and then I left. Of course she would never ask me for anything, nor did I ever suggest that she go see another physician. I did not even examine her as such, nor would she have accepted it. And there was no reason why I should, given the fact that I was always quite certain that Celina had no illness that either I or any other doctor would be able to cure.

Celina finally understood this. She encountered herself in her cats, in a primitive, childish, and strange way. She identified with them. She let herself be seduced by something which the cats embodied, made solidly, constantly present. Someone other than myself, someone less involved, less tied to the situation, someone who might perhaps have had a little more imagination—let us say, a spectator watching the situation from outside it—would have found something fantastic and suggestive in Celina's relationship with her cats, something susceptible of turning into the material of a story in which the terror and seductiveness of those dark surroundings created by Edgar Allan Poe would dominate. But I . . . what were these cats to me? Do they really have anything to do with what I have gone through? I feel a certain humiliation, as if against my will I am having to accept the truthfulness of an old superstition, of an irrational, inexplicable belief, or of an unknown reality.

And it is difficult for me to accept it. I have to force myself to think again about something that has nevertheless been present for such a long time. What had happened to me earlier when I was afraid Celina might have a lover, I now felt the first time one of those animals appeared in her room. I was jealous from then on. Really jealous. Jealous of the cats. Earlier it had been something else, perhaps simply, at bottom, the fact that I felt hurt. Now it was different. A secluded, painful anger was eating away pitilessly from within. The truth is that I had never felt anything with such reality and force. For years I had been living on the margins of myself, I had been looking on with a cool curiosity at what was happening as if I were unable to intervene at all. And now, suddenly . . .

I have never spoken about this with anyone. I am not close to anyone. (Was I ever close to Celina?) And even if I had been close to someone, who would I have been able to tell?

I knew, with a certitude that was odd because of the way it imposed itself upon me without my being able to avoid it, (nor did I wish to), I knew that Celina was unfaithful to me with the cats. She had no physical relations with them, I don't mean that. She wasn't even affectionate with them, nor did she pet them constantly as some women do particularly if they live alone and are no longer young. But she had an intimate, secretly shameless rapprochement with them. For the first time in my life I realized that animals live in a world of their own that is forbidden us, one in which we should never appear. But Celina shared in it. She lived in that world. That is where her infidelity lay. Celina had abandoned my world to shut herself up in another that was alien to me, one that I was unable and unwilling to penetrate. A world that, as I well understood, might have managed to exercise a somber attraction over me, one that I instinctively defended myself against, as one does who is in danger of perishing. The cats transmitted something to her, and she allowed them to do it; she lent herself, she served them as a vehicle, she had turned into the bearer of some iniquitous thing that I identified with evil, the abyss, sickness, and death.

Could I have been mistaken?

I have always lived too close to concrete things that can be proved, too close to processes where every effect has a cause that is able to be determined, to allow myself to be easily involved in the vagueness of an imprecise, contingent feeling. But nonetheless I believe in all that, and at the same time I would not be able to prove anything of what I witnessed, of what I am claiming here. I couldn't have proved it at that time, a year ago. I could have proved that Celina was not actually ill—that she had no organic illness, I mean—and in consequence that her confinement had something morbid, even mad, about it. I could also have proved that it is no everyday thing for a woman to shut herself up in her room with twelve cats, breaking off contact with the world, the true world, the outside world. I could have proved that and perhaps had her committed to a sanatorium where her confinement would have been justified and accepted. I could have gone somewhere else, left my patients behind, broken ties, started a new life. I could have continued with my old life, forgotten Celina, pretended as if she didn't exist. But no. I was not able to do any of those things, given the fact that I didn't do them, and that what I did do was a completely different thing.

I began to send her anonymous letters.

I really don't know how it occurred to me. I must have read about it somewhere. At one time I used to like mystery novels, and I was always fascinated by that improbable but at the same time scrupulously logical world in which all the threads come together and motives are structured with the inevitability of a diagnosis.

It was a childish scheme, one which at first I tried to get out of my mind as something intrusive, irrational, a vain, futile idea. Moreover, it was so petty that it disgusted me. Something not done by respectable people, especially a man. I told myself this a thousand times. This was the act of a woman, a jealous woman. But the project excited me; it was a stimulus that made me feel alive and able to act, to make decisions, take the initiative.

Eventually I sent the first of those letters, those ingenuous yet malevolent messages that very quickly turned into a necessity as ordinary as eating at fixed times or keeping my office hours from five to eight. My intention was to make Celina believe that I had a lover, that I was in love with someone else. That she enjoyed no dominion over me, that she had failed.

Day after day, everywhere I went, Celina's room pursued me: the half-light, the position of the furniture, the painting of the three women with their mantillas, the monstrously tiny sphinxes, and above all, that greenness: the green of the curtains, the canopy over the bed, the chairs—the greenish domination over the whole room which was in the light, the air, the cats' fur, on Celina's skin.

Until one morning when I left my car in front of the hospital, as I was closing the window and glancing mechanically at the seat beside me to verify that I hadn't left anything, a single image displaced all the rest. The bedroom was erased completely from mind as if it were a quick cut in a moving picture, and I saw only the body of Celina, Celina's dead body sprawled over the car seat, sprawled on her bed. Abruptly I shut the car door on Celina's dead body in order to erase it as well. But it stayed there.

I knew then that Celina was going to commit suicide. I realized that she had already known it, at least latently, for some time. I understood why I was sending her those letters. It was my small contribution. It was my ingenuous and pitiless way of intervening from a distance. I took the stairs at the hospital two at a time, very excited, as if I had just come across the tiniest, most elusive, and at the same time decisive piece of the puzzle, the piece that is always there in all those games and that is the key to rapidly putting in all the missing ones later on to form the figure.

I expected this without any anxiety. There was no doubt. It couldn't be any other way.

I didn't have to get accustomed to the idea. It had done nothing more than come to the surface, like a seed buried for a long time that has finally produced a perfect, complete plant.

Then I began to think about her bedroom as the site where this would have to take place, as the background chosen by Celina in order to surround her death. I didn't make sense of, and I still do not understand, the presence of that furniture (with its classical, Apollinean air that stands for the lucidity and transparency of the spirit) presiding over that dark ceremony, the secret, diabolical rite of suicide.

I can say that from that moment on, my life depended on Celina's death. It took greedy nourishment from the knowledge which allowed me to feel that what was happening to me was finally taking shape, was crystallizing around this fact that one day would be inalterable.

The rest scarcely changed. Except that I could no longer go on occupying my room in Celina's house, the bedroom separated from hers only by the bathroom door. I never slept there again. But I would go to see her. Not with any regularity, just at random, on no particular day, with the vague fear, or desire, or foreboding, of being received by Lydia or by the servant from the Phillipines who always met me at the door, this time with an upset expression on her face, not knowing how to break it to me that Madame, just a while ago, no one knew quite how . . .

I never thought it would be I myself, that the house would be so darkly silent, as distant as if it had never completely existed, that I would mount the stairs without turning on any lights, to open the door of her room expecting to find her asleep and be struck by the reddish brilliance from the rose-colored lampshade on her night table, that the blanket would cover her to the neck except for her arms, except for her bare arms on the coverlet, on the sheet, her arms the cats had been scratching at perhaps while attempting to awaken her or force her to pet them, that I would come nearer and nearer the better to see her up close, for the first time in ever so long, but now incapable of touching her, of feeling that strange tenderness and the desire to embrace her, that I was going to pick up the telephone mechanically to call the police and sit down nowhere but on the *chaise-longue* to wait for them. Or that I would be showing them the empty pill-bottle, and the cat scratches, that I would be giving them my address and putting myself at their disposal for anything that might be necessary, and that I would then leave her there alone with them.

It never occurred to me that it would happen last night. Nor that today, following last night, I would need to write all this. Would I be able to say, would I be able to tell anyone that it was I who killed Celina?

I was not there earlier last night, I mean. I didn't touch her. I never saw her until she was dead. If I were to say that I killed her, no one would believe me. They would never believe me. They, the ones who remained there last night after I left, the ones who perhaps are there even now, or else who never came back, the ones who did not find any necessity to call me this whole day long, nor to ask me anything else, nor to take me into account. The police. Nor anyone else. No one will believe me. I would like to be certain that they are unable to believe me because it is the truth, and the truth is always too easy and simple to be believed. But is it really the truth? Isn't it really that I need to believe it, to deceive myself, to think that it was I who destroyed Celina, to think that at least I hastened things, that I had something to do with it? Because if not, then Celina's death would be as if she had destroyed me.

Now there is nothing for me to do but hope, though I wouldn't know how to say what it is I can hope for.

Some day I will go to the house and remove all that furniture from Celina's room. But that is not important. Nothing is important now. Never to see Celina again! How can I bear it?

And now, after writing so many futile words, I will have to destroy them. Because if there is anything that should be preserved out of all this, that something should remain just between us. Between Celina and me. And the cats. Those cats who came to bring disorder, or rather, that is, who came to bring it to the surface, because I have to recognize that they introduced nothing new, nothing that was not already there, secret and larval, in Celina's nature.

If there was this fascination between Celina and the cats it was because, as it seems to me I have said before, Celina did nothing more than discover something of herself in the cats that so fascinated her.

Celina did nothing more than to surround herself with mirrors. But this should all remain between us. For this whole thing has a certain beauty. A beauty that depends so much on silence alone. And on oblivion.

The
Baptism

*F*or a moment it is Sunday. And lately Sundays are strange days that she would like to blot out of the week. Sundays have begun to be tinged with something dark, something that surrounds the name "Sunday" and makes it opaque as if, from one moment to the next, time might come to an end. Perhaps it is because everything is so quiet. Natalia doesn't want to think about it. She prefers not to remember that she is afraid of Sundays. Since when? She is not sure. That is another of the things that have been happening to her. She never knows anything very well, and she feels surprised and disconcerted every time someone says or denies anything with an air of certainty, as though there might be a huge quantity of indisputable truths. One day, staring at a square made by the sun shining on a patch of four tiles, she started to cry desperately. And every little while since then she breaks into tears no matter where she is. Especially if the wish suddenly comes over her to do something impossible, such as touching a treetop or walking suspended in midair. Things she cannot say to anyone because they would make fun of her.

The lawn is thick, hard, intensely green, with no

nuances. There is only the one difference of tone, but this one is quite marked, between the part where the sun shines on it and the part where the shade is. The shady green is damper, and the sunny green has something yellowish about it, a less emphatic green. At noon, the sun and the shade are perfect (it is only about things like this that one can be certain), so complete that if she hadn't been aware of other days, if she didn't know that the afternoon is infinitely full of changes, she might think that the way they are at that moment is the way they will be forever. For Natalia, holidays are special. What she feels on those days never happens on ordinary days. Only once did she not feel this way on a holiday, even though everyone kept telling her that that one, the day of her first communion, was the happiest day of her life. After she was told this, still quite early before she had begun to get dressed, of course something did change that turned it into a vaguely different sort of day, but not the happiest day of her life; it was simply a duration that didn't belong to her, an elusive, detached duration that had slipped away from her, that ended before its time.

Today is going to be different. A real holiday. Since scarcely a moment ago, this Sunday has been pushed aside into a place Natalia can no longer get to because she has quickly drawn a long chalk line into order to stay on this side of it, secure and protected. Today will be almost like a birthday. Almost, because a birthday has something about it from the moment you wake up, a restrained excitement that has been kept in reserve for the whole year in order to be expended without restraint on that exact day. Today Michel is going to be baptized.

Natalia takes off her shoes and stockings and hides them among the hydrangeas. How much longer will she have to wear these low, patent leather shoes with a tiny button instead of a buckle on the outer side? Her mother thinks that since she still likes dolls, since she loves Michel so much . . .

But she feels so tall, so tall; there's a good reason for them all to say that something must have been pulling her out at night. Sometimes when she walks around with nothing in her hands, as now, she would like to take her arms off and leave them somewhere. She doesn't know what to do with them. Then she starts to think: she has a stomach and a spinal column, but more than anything she has a face. And it's so bothersome to know one has a face and everyone else can recognize her, while she can only see herself with her own eyes when she looks in the mirror.

It's strange to feel how wet her feet are and the sharp, biting grass beneath her soles. She runs with her eyes shut. But first she has estimated the distance well, and so she is certain there is no danger. But suddenly she takes fright and knows without the slightest doubt that she is going to run into a huge tree trunk and suffer an unspeakable pain in the middle of her face, that she is going to get her nose and eyes smashed in, that she will be terribly disfigured, covered with blood. She has to open her eyes right then.

The morning is completely yellow. Several shadowy disks come between her eyes and that intense yellow. To get rid of them she presses her eyelids down with the tips of her fingers but only manages to get them to grow larger and smaller, until she makes a great effort to keep her eyes open and finally the shadows disappear. The color is the same. The same as it was that day when she woke up feeling she was still dreaming and that only by getting up and finding some proof of it somewhere else would she be able to be convinced of being awake. Then she got up and began to walk through the whole house until she came to her mother's room. There the sun shone differently upon the window, and her mother was seated before the dresser combing out her hair, and the sun gave her skin another color, a soothing, deep tone. Natalia could not contain herself and ran to give her a kiss and sit in her lap, refusing to leave until she received a kiss in return.

Michel is a baby, tiny and soft. She has had him ever since she can remember. It was just a few days ago that it occurred to them to have him baptized. Or rather, it occurred to Marisa, to her aunt who looks so much like her mother that people all think they are twins when she isn't even her sister but her cousin, and she's younger, too, a little younger than her mother.

She likes to stay like this for a long time, lying down on her back. The garden seems much larger, especially because the ground slopes down right there and makes this bank like a small hill she sometimes rolls down, where everything is so open as if their garden didn't end in order for the neighbors' garden to begin. The house can be seen very far away, bigger, a house that is not totally the same one she has just come out of, a house that even so is much more hers now than when she is there inside it with the others, amid the sounds of cleaning and the songs of the servants. A house that is hers just as if she had but a moment ago built it herself out of the old set of blocks she never plays with any more, with the small columns, the arches, the windows with the red cellophane instead of glass, the squares and triangles of different colors; a house that she could touch if she wished, if she decided to open her hands wide and then enclose it inside her palms, just for her very own. It looks as though it had only recently been set down upon the grass, without cement, as if last night the space where it now is had still been empty. From there she sees the whole house, with the terrace and the stairs in front and a similar terrace and stairs in back; the windows, so many windows in a line from one side to the other, allowing the white curtains to be seen, pulled back to each side; and up above, two other balconies, and the same windows—so square, so symmetrical, as only houses are that are built for playing in. If it should rain it would get very dark inside and the lights behind some of the windows would be turned on. She would stay where she is, but only for a moment, because she can't stand wearing a wet dress that sticks to her back, and she would have to run inside to take shelter, change clothes, and station herself to watch the rain from behind the glass windows that she now sees from below, and then to have the itch up there to go back out into the rain, to throw herself into the pond to feel the warm water all around like when you are in the ocean and it starts raining.

(There is also another kind of rain, the rain that gathers in the hallways at school, that reveals the filthiness of the old tiles, that floods the patio and slowly fills her with fear as if it were building a wall around her that would turn solid and hard in order to keep her from getting out, escaping, and going home to her own house, behind the glass window, watching this different rain that protects her, makes the pond overflow and creates pools on the lawn: the rain that is not heard and that darkens the street and does not allow anyone to see beyond the grating, the empty street, and the house so far away across the street.)

But it is not raining now. Nothing disturbs the water in the pond. She might put her hand out maybe and with the tips of her fingers touch the long, slippery stem of a purplish flower, one that has now fallen down over the round leaves with the thorns on them. There is no wind, not the slightest breeze. The palm leaves are not moving, nor the shrubs without flowers, nor the white, pink, and lilac-colored oleanders. It is very hot. Where she is lying in the shade of the hydrangea patch, the heat surrounds her like an invisible wave just on the verge of breaking over her. The silent ring advances without a sound but charged with tension as if the smooth lawn and the neat masses of shrubs and flowers were concealing the ubiquitous, crouching presence of an unknown wild beast. It is all very hazy to Natalia, with her somewhat bewildered curiosity that causes her to observe in minute detail everything surrounding her as

if at any moment she might discover something else somewhere, something mysterious and secret. The heat climbs
sluggishly up her legs and seems built in, just as if it is coming
out of her skin, until the sweat gradually dampens her, relaxes
her, and she feels as though her legs are not hers. Maybe that
is why it does not occur to her that she could move, change
places, seek out some other place where the shade might last a
little longer, although from between her half-closed eyes she is
lazily contemplating it a short distance away, where the semi-
circles spread out around the tall, abundant foliage. The sun
strikes her right in the eye, and it makes her see everything as
if surrounded by an irridescent aureole, a second nature, as if
each leaf, each tree trunk, the edge of the lake, the water plants,
the grass, and in the distance the whole house, but especially
the sun, the sun beating down on her head from the middle of
the pale sky, were secreting a substance capable of extending
them beyond their own limits in order to give them an appearance at once more indisputable and more fantastic, more
present and more strange, more real and more unreal.

The boiling atmosphere is heavy around her, becoming gradually more solid, with a consistency that would seem
not to be made of air but of a more compact body, maybe water
in fact, yes, especially of water, in such a way that something
is resounding in her ears, a muffled, opaque sound that one
might feel when lying on the bottom, completely covered
beneath the surface of the water. Beyond her, the garden, the
house, on a level that is different from the one which seems to
be coming from her own ears, are other diverse sounds mixed
in, that mingle indistinctly with each other in a vague, diffuse,
irregular rhythm. After the silence that is so thick and penetrating, the sound that is not its absence but its natural prolongation, its condensation, a sound that negates itself, that is made
of the accumulated silence. That is why Natalia scarcely
perceives the difference; she accommodates herself easily,

allows it to blend without transition into the quality of the ambience, which has gradually acquired sonority until she herself seems to be vibrating and transmitting the sound. She needs to remain quiet in order to listen and feel herself listening, to receive the signals emanating from things, those signals that she discovered one day when she was much younger as she gazed at the long street, the enormously long, empty street without the slightest bit of sunlight nor brightness about it, the smooth, strange street one Sunday, another Sunday, in the afternoon. In those days they were not living in this house close to the lake but in the old house in the center of the city, on the street where the streetcars ran. A street named San Lázaro, close to the ocean. Natalia shuts her eyes again and allows herself to float on that watery consistency that surrounds her, contains her, possesses her, but she cannot wholly distance herself from the balcony, that balcony from which she watches the endless street with its four streetcar tracks, the cables on a level with the balconies, those white-and-yellow, yellow-and-white balconies, the white-or-black iron balconies repeating themselves to infinity along that street. She has just returned from the movies, from a motion picture about pirates and islands full of beaches and palm trees. Without seeing it, she has walked down the long street, barren of streetcars and almost of people. Afterward she goes out on that balcony and looks at the street. And for the first time, she sees it. The empty street. Empty, but living. Detached from everything else, from the other streets approaching her and leading away from her, detached from the moments during which it is a street filled with people, cars, and streetcars, detached from the many mornings and afternoons she has traversed the street going to and from school, detached from everything except its smooth, lengthy surface and its houses, the two threads of buildings that mark its limits equally on both sides, reduced to the traits that make them alike—their balconies, their cornices a little below the level of the rooftops—and excluding everything that makes one house different from the next. The street is there as if the whole world were reduced to it and it embraced the whole world, turned into the only street, into the most street-like street of all that ever were and could ever have been in any part of an inexhaustible extension without limits, as is the world for Natalia. That street has remained static, as in a photograph, rejecting all movement. Natalia, standing on the balcony, thinks she is recording that fixedness as if she herself were a camera. That is why she is so quiet there on the balcony, here in the garden behind the hydrangeas, so that all this can be engraved, this sensation that she might almost be able to touch and that fills her with joy and is nothing other than the certitude that the street and the garden exist in a definitive manner and that neither—then it was the street, now the garden—will ever be able to return to the place of Natalia's premonitions, where things have not yet begun to exist, where she too, of course, where even she must have been at one time.

The assurance of being afloat on a formless moving surface where things, before existing like the garden, like the street, fuse together and are lost. Natalia, in her refuge, becomes the street of that afternoon again, she is the garden of this morning, she allows them a place within her that is so big that there is no longer anything but a tiny corner left for her, a hiding place were she has to get down on her knees and scruntch herself down to be able to see them and at the same time allow them the freedom of the whole space, to permit them to fill it up, to take possession of it and eliminate it and turn it into a memory in a part of her very self that no longer will let her be alone, that will be company for her every time she is afraid—afraid of anything, afraid of nothing, afraid of dying.

There is peace now, a peace that soothes things, that is in the lighter air, in the breeze that blows from time to time because the most intensely charged point of noon is already passing and the heat is refining itself, losing its heaviness, opening up to the breeze, spreading itself around.

Natalia sits up and looks around. The lawn descends gently from the other side of the house to the lake. The fence that goes entirely around the garden is smaller there so as not to interrupt the view, so the lake can seem part of the extensive yard of the house. Since the area where the fence runs is also the lowest point of the slope, one can easily jump over it to the other side. The huge palm trees, all separate from each other, rise from the middle of the lawn's open spaces, encircled by climbing vines whose leaves are shot through with holes or else jagged and irregular, but some of the palms stand up smooth and solitary without any entangling growth.

Since the palm trees grow in the middle of the lawn and there are no other trees to cast their shade on it, the grass has the same freshness all over. Natalia thinks it is a perfect garden, like the gardens in books, a garden where she can shut out the world and not need anything else. Everything is reduced to being there inside it, on this side of the fence, knowing that she will not have to leave it, that she has not come just for the visit, that this unique place surrounded by a high iron fence is hers, all hers. Still, she would like to leave. To leave and shut the gate and put her face up to the bars and look inside as if she were some other person, to pretend as though it were not she but someone else passing along the street, a little girl perhaps whose name is not Natalia, who does not live in this house, who is not having a holiday today, who does not have a doll named Michel.

They have been calling her for some time. She likes to let them shout, to pretend as though she doesn't hear. She likes to hear "Natalia" called out this way, with the second "a" prolonged, almost sung, as it always sounds when she is being called from a distance.

She would be able to sleep for hours in this very spot where she is now, with her face into the hydrangeas, hearing them call out "Natalia," letting herself be sung to sleep at length, interminably, by that familiar music, by the affectionate, chanted pronunciation of her name, which would be transformed at some moment to end in that whispering, almost silent "Natalia" with which her mother, seated by her bedside, puts her to sleep every night, since before there was a beginning; she still puts her to sleep because time has not passed and she is six or perhaps even four and the milk-glass lamp with the sketches on it is lit and her mother finally puts it out and in the darkness are heard the cicadas and the night comes softly to an end.

By three o'clock, Natalia could wait no longer; the party was going to begin at five. They had come out to the garden to wake her up. Fanny, tired of calling her, of shouting for her from the kitchen, crossed the grass to look for her by the side of the pond, behind the hydrangeas. She always seemed in a bad humor but that really was so only when speaking to her in English, saying, "Naughty girl, can't she ever do what she is told?" Natalia could not bear to be spoken to in this way as if she were being forced to obliterate herself completely behind that impersonal "she," taking it almost like an insult.

But she was used to Fanny, just as she was to that room upstairs where she was always served her meals, with the three amber-colored windows looking out over the stairway into the house, and the other windows, also with wrinkly, amber-colored glass, over the garden. The best place in the house. The wicker furniture for the most part was comprised of rocking chairs. To enter that room at any hour of the day was equivalent to passing from ordinary everyday life into a much more real place, to begin to form part of a story for telling or to enter a painting with a gilded background and there become an angel in profile, hands together and praying, or a roly-poly blonde baby Jesus seated on the thighs of a Virgin. It was a magic place that whenever she wished could become transformed into the cabin of a ship plowing through the ocean in the midst of a storm, or into the jungle traversed by an explorer named Alvar Núñez Cabeza de Vaca, the only survivor of a shipwreck, a name filled with distance and mystery that inhabited Natalia's imagination with a radiant reality as only the characters out of fantasy do. The room was neither square nor rectangular but a kind of semicircle or half moon. Most likely—Natalia, at any rate, liked to think so—there was no other room like this anywhere. There was never the slightest danger there, nothing unpleasant could ever happen, and even the most inoffensive things that were taking place outside it—like the comings and goings of the servants as they were cleaning, or the arrival of an itinerant peddler, or Ney the police dog's barking and racing about—would take on another character, another significance, seeming to complete something that could not be explained (Natalia couldn't explain it to herself) but that was taking shape there within the room and then would slide outward from it like a huge spider web all made of gold. To enter that room was to settle oneself within an ambience where everything was foreseen or where the only things that happened were things that had already taken place and that for this reason must follow an assured process toward an inevitable end, with no surprises. For Natalia it was the possibility of reproducing the stimulating sensation, the excitement that for the past two or three years books had been giving her, a few books, that is, that she would read over and over again. The impression of touching something unknown, of skirting another, much richer world that harbored a promise which would never vanish because it had never been completely revealed.

To wait there until time for the party after having taken as long as possible over lunch was almost impossible. Natalia couldn't think of a pretext. But to stay there was to assure the party a protected space, a privileged place and time to the side of those places and times where at any moment things can get away from you and vanish.

Perhaps because the light in that room (which was not really anything exactly, not a dining room, nor a living room, nor a bedroom, nor a terrace) was always golden at any hour, Natalia chased everywhere after the changes in the coloration of the light until she encountered a peculiar yellow hue that somehow would bring back the atmosphere of enchantment of that place. In the garden that morning this approximate color, which she had suddenly come across by surprise, had assured her the perfection of the day, of the afternoon and the party, and had been enough to suppress any recollected fears, any tiny anticipated distress. Now, more than the party itself, she would like to remain there and think about it, to live freely the anticipation of the party, to foretell it and make it up as she wished, allowing no detail to get away from her nor permitting anything to depart in the slightest from the course she would choose and arrange.

After meticulously cleaning up the bread crumbs, Fanny picked up the tablecloth and folded it in a perfect square before putting it away in one of the drawers of the small piece of wicker furniture of indefinite color that opened on both sides, the same one that had served as a storage place for her baby clothes.

"Now it's time to get dressed. We have to be ready to greet the guests."

Fanny always knew what was supposed to be done and she was never mistaken. She lived among calendars, clean uniforms, and games governed by rules, a world that surrounded Natalia's world where the probabilities were infinitely fluctuating and variable, as around a securely anchored pier at which any moment now one might possibly arrive. It was a resource that was there, was available, precisely because Natalia preferred not to make use of it, not to come too close, remaining instead at a prudent distance, as if floating amid the swelling waves on a raft that found no merit in seeking the shelter of terra firma. To tell Fanny that they should remain there and talk about the party and thus with their words put together a kind of indestructible magic charm in order to keep the true party alive every moment would be useless because Fanny would never agree that the party was anything other than the arrival of the guests, the tea, and the baptismal ceremony, for which a friend of her father would dress as the priest and her Aunt Marisa and her own father would be the godparents, and afterward would come the games in the garden and the prizes. Fanny's party would last from five until seven. For Natalia, on the other hand, the party consisted of the anticipation, the preparations, the focussing of all the intensity accumulated throughout the day, this premonition of something quite whole, complete, and shining that had been slowly and gradually crystallizing.

"Don't you want to go down to see everything?"

Natalia knew that Fanny would be able to drag her brusquely out of her dreams in order to transport her to a place where the objects were solid and opaque, where words became opaque too and bounced around like hollow spheres within an enormously huge, empty space. She made an effort to distance herself from that opacity, and the idea of going down to see everything then turned into an avalanche of infinite, minuscule sensations that a countless number of people in an endless number of unknown places in the whole world might be having at that very moment. She thought of Newfoundland and Tierra del Fuego, Alaska and New Zealand, and these last two words conjured up a bluish, translucent brightness as if it were a case of an island merely imagined in a remote and unattainable region of the air. Without saying the words she repeated them

several times in Spanish: "*Nueva Zelandia. Nueva Zelandia.*"
And then in English: "New Zealand. New Zealand," buzzing
silently and prolonging the "z," savoring the slippery sound of
the syllable that was turning into the unusually white foam of
waves beating upon the sand.

"New Zealand. New Zealand. Do you know where
New Zealand is, Fanny? Do you know where it is?"

Fanny paid no attention; she merely pushed the little
table Natalia had eaten from against the wall and disappeared
into the room beside it, which was Natalia's room. She came
back right away and, in a cold, clear tone, as if that were the
correct one, and as if she had not said the almost the same thing
a few moments previously, she announced:

"You must be all dressed within half an hour. You have
to greet the guests."

Natalia saw herself at the top of the staircase, among
the palms, greeting each guest with a graceful curtsy, as the
little princesses do in the movies. Her mother and Fanny would
be smiling in approval.

Before, she used to take pleasure in that small ceremony; it filled her with a special gratification, as if she had
ceased being herself in order to play a small role that could only
be entrusted to her. But now she was incapable—and she
would be so throughout the whole infinite time of the future—
of ever again pausing at the top of the staircase and repeating
twenty or thirty or forty times the same gesture she used to
enjoy, that had turned her into the center of all attention and
made her think so eagerly every Christmas, without knowing
why, of the joy of getting ready for the birth.

She got up and followed Fanny. But she didn't walk
down the stairs behind her; instead she let herself slide as she
had not done for who knows how long along the marble
bannister, always so cold and slippery. Fanny didn't let on that
she was aware of it and continued her descent with her usual

step—as if she were marching—and only when Natalia got all the way down to where Fanny was already waiting for her did the latter say in English the words that were to be expected of her, but with a certain lack of enthusiasm and speaking only because she could not fail to say them:

"You're a big girl now, Natalia . . ."

The kitchen shone. Everything was overwhelmingly white and brilliant. The sun came in violently through the blinds and in between the two windows formed a nucleus where both light and heat at once reverberated. Around that sunny center everything gave the impression of floating just as if the tables, the chairs, the tile counters, and the dishes resting on them were not absolutely fixed but instead were rather feebly secured to the unsettled consistency of the atmosphere. Natalia would have wanted to throw herself into that circle of light as into the waters of the pond. She shut her eyes for a moment the better to hear the sound of the sharpened knife that Marta the cook was using to cut the last bits of different-colored greens for putting into the salad.

Marta let her taste the mayonnaise. Natalia took up a little of the yellow sauce on the tip of a spoon and placed it carefully on her tongue, ready to taste it, but allowing the slightly acid taste which homemade mayonnaise always had to rest there before swallowing it down. Afterward she gradually filled up the spoon, drawing shapes in the sauce as it stuck to the glass, and greedily took in the creamy liquid. She went on poking around, looking for something familiar on every dish, mentally reproducing the taste of each thing, dishes of which it could not be said that she knew them very well or that she kept them in her memory, because there was something more: they were completely integrated into herself as if they formed part of her own organism or else as if each time they reappeared they found a track traced there so often that they were immediately assimilated.

Natalia stared at her mother, seated before the long table that occupied the whole center of the kitchen, and it seemed to her that she had always been sitting there, in exactly the same position, separated from her by the shaft of light that blurred her outlines in such a way that she was surrounded by a kind of aureole. Seeing her this way, it was impossible for Natalia to think she could ever have been anywhere else, not only at this moment but at any time. Oh, if only she wouldn't say anything. If only she would remain silent. If only she wouldn't shatter the perfection of that moment. If only she wouldn't cease moving her hand back and forth, brushing the rolls with exactly the same rhythm, never faltering even once. Natalia recognized the same sensation she had had this morning in the garden, the one that had brought on the recollection of the street filled with balconies. Now she would have liked to have a camera to really take a picture, so she wouldn't have to be content to rely only on herself for recording what she was looking at and fixing it definitively. Things and people seemed to be pursuing her that day as if there were nothing else for it but to encounter them, to be gazing at them.

At that moment Natalia would not have been able to explain herself to anyone. She would only have been able to do something in desperation such as shout to the four winds that she was there to gather up everything, to understand everything, to want everything, to receive everything.

Natalia is running. She is running through the garden and she would like to have the courage to open the gate and leave it. Or to jump over the fences that are down the slope at the other end and make her way past the pond without knowing where she was going. No one notices her. The party is a racket of confused, strident voices that she would like to leave behind just as she would leave the afternoon behind if she could. Her hands are damp and she feels her dress as a tiresome thing stuck to her skin, as a second skin that is so uncomfortable and intrusive, so irritating that she would also like to take it off. Then, without the afternoon, without the party, without the dress, she would not be exposed to anything any more and she might begin another day again that perhaps would be perfect, a day when she would be waiting for the party to begin, when nothing extraordinary would have to happen, and she could put together a party in her own way, any party—far away and unlikely—or else a day when the hours would go by without rushing, as if they were not going by at all, hours filled with nothing else than themselves, with that impalpable material that is like an irrational, intense joy, an unjustified but definitive fulsomeness.

In the darkness the two figures are fused into each other. Bound together, they seem like one. That single form remains motionless and then it moves, hesitates, takes on peculiar outlines until it is transfigured into two distinct shadows, two heads, two bodies scarcely separated. Mechanically she draws near the clump of hydrangeas, perhaps only because she had been there that morning, or because it is her favorite place in the whole garden, her refuge, the corner where she can always hide for long periods without being bothered.

She does not know why, but while Michel is being baptized she has an urge to to tell them all that the idea was not hers, that it would never have occurred to her, that they should excuse her but it all seems so foolish, or worse, something ugly, unpleasant, sad. When she sees the priest come out and then Luis and Marisa so seriously, she carrying the doll with its long baptism gown, he beside her, she feels she is witnessing something else, not a game but perhaps a farce where nothing is for laughing. Marisa and Luis are carrying a real little boy, flesh and blood, a child of theirs, and Natalia has no place there. Any moment now they could tell her to go away, not to bother them, that the house will no longer be hers, the garden no longer hers, nor will she be able to go to sleep on the grass, nor anything.

   The people begin to arrive because it is a little past five. A moment ago she has stopped for some time in front of the mirror, looking at herself intently hoping to find out what she really is like, whether she is pretty or ugly, but she has seen nothing but the small white flowers of embroidered fabric, the strawberry-colored velvet ribbon with its long ends reaching down to the hem of her dress, that other ribbon that Fanny has put in her hair to pull it back because that is the way the young ladies do it. Fanny says she looks like a "lady," using the English word, which splits apart into all its letters and Natalia counts them and thinks there must be five, and feels pleased that she knows how "lady" is spelled and wishes—the opposite of the other times—that Fanny would talk to her in English. It is strange that this face she sees in the mirror does not look like her face, and that she does not know if it is pretty or ugly, she does not know if the guests will recognize her, or whether they won't know who it is when they see her because she might be anyone, because there is nothing that sets her apart.

   Immediately there is the whirlwind of the arrivals, the gifts, of opening them, showing them around, putting them on view on the lace bedspread which her grandmother made fifty years ago, or her great grandmother a hundred, on top of this thing that seems about to fall apart, that looks like the veil of a bride of a hundred years ago.

   Natalia is suffocating. She touches her brow with an automatic gesture as she if thought she might have a fever. It is fully nighttime now, and the voices have ceased to be heard.

   For the first time in her life she has been given flowers: carnations, roses, lilies of the valley. The guests keep arriving gradually, and she has to go down and back up again, go up and back down, all the time. She receives each gift and says, "How nice," and hears the comments and smiles the whole time without stopping, without knowing for whom. Then she is told the baptism is about to begin, and she runs down so as not to miss anything. It is going to be a lot of fun. Especially because she sees it all a little from the outside knowing that this is the last time for something (though ignorant of what that thing is), perhaps the final act of a performance that must already have gone on too long. Behind the last palm trees, the sky takes on a pale amber color that gradually turns orange-colored and then red, while the white clouds, nearly frayed out, turn grey just above where everyone is gathered and immediately blend into the rest of the sky. It occurs to Natalia that the sky has never been exactly that color at this hour, perhaps never in all the times since the world began. Thinking this brings her the exciting sensation of discovery. So she is happy, extraordinarily happy, because of the breeze, the noise, the people, as if everything were coming together before her until forming a remarkably high flight of stairs she would be able to climb in a moment to contemplate the world from up there.

And then, from one moment to the next, everything becomes opaque. Exactly as if this were a stage set and suddenly the scene went dark in order to change the backdrop and the characters were changing costumes and even their roles. The gestures lose all sense of proportion, become exaggerated, seem like overdone grimaces, and the words are lost in a gigantic hole that seems to be empty of anything. Unable to take her eyes off it, Natalia stares at the movements of a red and black bird that is flying, wings beating, but without moving from its place above a quiet sea. Marisa and Luis. The two infinitely heavy names, like lead, are dragging her to the ground without allowing her to move.

The lights have been turned on inside the house but the garden is an indistinct dark mass where the colors of the flowers and leaves are indistinguishable. There is a little breeze, and Natalia feels that it is cooling her off because she is sweating and a shiver runs through her. She cannot go back to the house and look at their faces. If only no one remembers her. She would like to bring a lot of memories together in order to eradicate the most recent one and try to do something with them, to compose them in some way so they are able to form one solid, resistant day and she will be in the middle of it, as she saw a unicorn once in a book surrounded by a dense, enclosing, impenetrable hedge. But they are so few and delicate, so fleeting that they cannot be piled up to build anything around her; instead they scatter and fly around dizzily like tiny pieces of paper tossed into the wind. They fly about on all sides and the balconies become lost, the street, the streetcars, the pirates in the movie, the beaches of Nueva Zelandia and the sea, all the seas, and the amber light in the room upstairs, and the image of her mother in the white oh so white kitchen, and the rain that might have fallen but did not the whole day long, and the wet corridor at school, and the image of a different little girl behind the bars of the garden gate, gazing at everything from the outside. None of that is firm. Nothing works to help build up a tower of hard, thick bricks where she can go to sleep and forget, and that later on she can take with her everywhere, surrounding her always, so that no one will be able to come too close to her, no one will be able to hurt her.

They are behind the clump of hydrangeas. Their shadows are. Luis and Marisa, clasped in each other's arms, talking to each other in words she cannot manage to hear, while there in the house—so far away, so distant—everyone is bidding her mother goodbye and surely they are asking for her, but she will be unable to go in, unable to say goodbye to anyone, to say a single word, unable to stand the light and the looks. It is true that she has not dared to get closer, that she has not actually seen them, that she has no proof, that it has been nothing but a premonition, but this way is enough for her to know it, to imagine it; that moment in the middle of the ceremony was enough, the moment when she understood everything, and then that fused image behind the hydrangeas. Enough.

But she will not be able to stay here. She will have to go back. She will have to face them. Natalia clutches desperately at her morning, at the radiant noon, at that yellow light that follows her and that she chases after everywhere she goes. There has to be something solid in that, something firm somewhere, because everything else around her is coming undone, is fleeing from her, abandoning her, leaving her there by herself standing in the middle of the garden, in what used to be her garden because the garden is no longer anything either but an intense though incurably lost desire to be happy forever.

All the
Roses

*A*urelia is fondling the page of the calendar, sliding her fingers softly over the thick surface of the numerals, going over them affectionately, examining them. The yellowed page has a silky feel, almost velvet-like, and her finger slips along without finding any roughness. AUGUST 20, 1933. Underneath, the rest of the pages of the calendar appear intact, useless, without ever having served to set forth a precise time for anyone, to mark the numbered boundaries of each day and night, the certainty of a few indisputable hours for everyone. No. To suggest something that is like a limitless postponement, a duration in suspense, always similar to itself, that is mistaken for eternity, this never torn-out yellow page is enough, this piece of fragile paper where an arrested temporality is condensed, where the frontiers with the past and with the future are lost in the prolongation of an interminable present that blends memory and oblivion. For Aurelia, it has never stopped being the 20th of August, 1933, but what occurred that day, that is, if anything took place at all, has been absolutely eradicated from her mind. She only remembers, every morning there in front of the calendar, that on that 20th of August the others went away with such haste that they never even saw what date it was, perhaps because something happened very far away, somewhere else, or very close by in the city, this very city: something sinister, or something that filled them with jubilation, or, most probably, something violent and irreversible, as those events are that force people to drop everything and go away.

Aurelia recalls suddenly that all the roses are going to die. All the rosebushes. Maybe she has known this for days or perhaps years. Or since barely a second ago, when she began to fondle the outsized blue numerals on the yellowed calendar page. Thus this strange, sudden apprehension runs through her like a chill, this realization that was at first only a vague intuition and that now obsesses her, penetrates her and fills her, until she feels herself empty of everything but this, the coming death, the inevitable agony of the dying roses.

Perhaps if she were to tear out that page, rip it apart and destroy it, the rosebushes would cease dying. Perhaps if she were to go looking for a pencil to cross out that number 20 with two heavy lines, Alda would not be insane now, her slow death in the midst of her madness would stop, in the locked room that she, Aurelia, does not wish to enter. The city would stop pestering her on all sides, would stop drawing stealthily near the windows at night, would no longer whistle so protractedly at her through the slats of the blinds pushed ajar by the winds, it would stop pushing down on the roof like a gigantic bird perched atop the highest part of the house and harassing her with a sound that never stops, as if the ocean were nearby, this sound you could cut with a pair of scissors or tear apart as you would rip out the calendar page, because it is like paper, an enormous piece of paper that someone is constantly tearing apart in his hands. The city. The city that surrounds the house with a murmuring so hoarse, or sharp, or sibilant, like the crackling of a huge bonfire sometimes, perhaps the sound of the sun as it burns the rocks, a vibration that beats in the outside air and tries to violate the walls and blinds, tries to slip into the protected shadows where Aurelia trembles slightly as she recalls that the rosebushes are in danger, and that a secret curse which only she, she alone, has foreseen hangs heavily over them. The city, the labyrinth that has been voluntarily pushed into the realm of forgetfulness for who knows how long. The city that only turns benign, generous, something to be desired, when it ceases being this pressure that drives one to despair, this surreptitious, whistling presence that Aurelia watches over without a break, glueing her ear to the wall just in case, and that blends with other cities superimposed within her: rivers among cypresses and bridges the color of ancient topaz, behind which rise up towers and cupolas, statues that are white in the streets, arcades, columns, patios filled with flowers, little plazas forever lost when one turns the corner, huge plazas to which one descends by way of a narrow stairway at the end of an ancient street, white churches whose beauty is excessive, more than enough for them, a beauty that seems to emanate from the silent bell towers and come down to rest upon the tiles of the cloisters, the fountains, the streets of gray cobblestones and the long, luminous roads lined with pine trees. And with mansions, many mansions, with high balconies and terraced gardens, palazzos such as this one which is her own house, exactly like this one that someone moved here, brought here stone by stone, marble by marble, banister by banister, from a street in Florence, also full of heat and noise, but very old, solemn, and too sober, to the city that Aurelia has tried so to forget, the feminine, tropical city, dizzy with colors and scrolls, with columns and cupolas, to the garden of the tallest palm trees, Caribbean pines, and bougainvillea.

Aurelia looks around her and it is easy to return the house to its origins, to a pacifying murmur, to the freshness of a far-off autumn, to the ancientness of a street where it must have been accompanied by others just like it, and looking not at all distinct or odd alongside buildings smothered amid balconies, stained-glass windows, and cornices of plaster. Then she can eradicate the violence of the siege that this other city, the real one, the now city, has laid against the house, the siege of noise and heat, of a presence that is too dense, as if the whole outer world beyond the stone walls were inhabited by a huge savage beast always on the verge of lashing out with its paws, on the verge of sinking its claws precisely into the weakest spot, into the most fragile place in the structure, in order to provoke its deafening fall, the collapse of the palace over the big salon below, which she is contemplating from the second floor balcony that goes around it in such a way that the lower floor, the whole length of the hall, has no ceiling until that of the next floor above it, where hangs the chandelier which will also fall and be turned into thousands of pieces of shattered glass.

It is all so quiet . . . The artfully worked ceiling, the empty salon, the exceptionally white staircase with its broad landings, the silent books in the library, and the innumerable chairs in the long dining room, also silent. Aurelia closes her eyes the better to feel the silence, to let herself float in this air of absences that fills the house, to let herself be vacant, remembering nothing at all. She likes to feel herself empty like this. She immerses herself infinitely in that profound hollow that is gradually consuming her, gently, softly, like a warm, watery, endless funnel. A pleasure, vertigo, intoxication. Everything is becoming calm, and the happiness can be immense. Until something shakes her up, awakens her, forces her to open her eyes and look around, to wonder where she is, to rest her gaze wearily, beneath her heavy eyelids, on the quiet, dense objects, mysteriously dense, that address her with a mute, incomprehensible summons.

She has forgotten everything, but she does not know what it is she has forgotten. She does not know what she ought to remember. No matter that she tries for the recollection occasionally, that she pursues it eagerly, attempts to surround it, corner it, pester it, the way she feels that this strange city outside is surrounding the palazzo, laying siege to it, trying to overwhelm it. No matter that she fondles the yellowed calendar page every morning until she is weary of it. Nor that she repeats, under her breath as if in a litany, the name of the day, the month, the year, the saint's name, the meaningless sentence that is written below it in very tiny letters. It does not matter if she asks Lucila, if she threatens her with throwing her out of the house if she doesn't tell her, if she doesn't help her to recall what it is she is supposed to know, something that she would remember were it not for this spell cast over her, because maybe someone has given her the evil eye, because she is cursed in the same way as the roses dying in the garden. Lucila. Lucila. Lucila should be coming. She should ask her how Alda is, how she felt this morning. Whether she recognizes her when she goes into the room to take her meals in or give her medicines, whether she has asked for her, whether she has wondered why she never comes to see her, whether she blames her. To ask Lucila, to imagine, to think that what she is imagining is what is happening at that precise moment there within, inside the room where only Lucila goes, where she herself does not wish to appear, Alda's room.

Alda's room is dark. It is always dark. Alda is alone. She spends whole hours alone. There is no one to come and be company for her. No one. Not even Lucila, because she only goes in to do the cleaning, and—several times a day—to do first one thing, then another, and then something else, because she, Aurelia, has ordered her to. She has ordered her to do all those things that she herself should be able to do because Alda is her sister and it ought to be her duty; and it is, or it would be if everything had not changed, if she herself didn't have to take such care to protect herself from the infection, in order to go on living. Above all, now that everyone else has left. (Now?) Alda does not leave her room since they went away. She has never seen her walking through the house, and both have remained alone, Alda (the other one) secluded in the room that opens out onto the garden, onto that corner of the garden where the roses are dying, and she (Aurelia) is forced to pass through the house from one end to the other every day, morning, noon, and sometimes night, because she knows that something is going to happen if she stops doing this, and she has to count the steps as she goes around that endless railing that surrounds the salon, so that they are the same every time, neither more nor less, and then she must go into the dining room and reassure herself that all the glasses are in the cupboard, and check over the tassels on the rugs and later on go through the small drawing room with its gilded furniture. The same drawing room where her other sister, the one that left, would write letters all the time, except when visitors came, or she was combing her hair, or playing the piano, that languid, shining music that now is heard again, that Aurelia hears rising until it blends with the murmuring of words and laughter, just like a single, prolonged rustling of feminine voices, linked gently to the intensely sweet melody of the piano. The servants take the tea around, while Aurelia goes from one chair to another, from one rocker to the next, in order not to leave anybody out because she does not want to miss a single detail, and moreover because she cannot keep herself quiet, nor has she ever been able to remain seated in one place for very long. It is true that these are not her friends but Alda's, but that is not important. She likes them as well, she adores everyone and enjoys going down early before they arrive, taking her photo album, the pictures from the trip around the world, to show them one by one, explaining them, illustrating with an anecdote the ones that were taken in nameless, unidentifiable places, with the recollection of some unusual thing that had happened right when the snapshot was taken, exactly at that moment, or five minutes before or after, something trivial that acquired significance only through its having happened in relation to the fact that someone, her husband or someone they didn't know who was passing by there accidentally and whom they had asked to take a picture of both of them together, had chosen the place and the moment for taking the picture, and moreover had allowed himself to make that choice only in order to transmit something. Aurelia thinks of each of these possibilities, vaguely, as she rules out all the rest except for the afternoon reception, the guests, the music, and the snapshots in the album.

There is the album, within arm's reach. She only needs to walk a few steps and open the upper drawer of the chiffonier in order to be able to take it in her arms and caress it, just as she fondles the calendar figures. She has already risen to go look for it. She is as excited as if she were in love with someone at this moment. She thumbs through the pages, calmly, as if she were not looking for anything in particular. Why is that? All the snapshots are just alike. But, moreover, she doesn't need to get up. She won't get up. She has the album there, in her lap, she always takes it with her, for fear that if she puts it away she won't be able to remember later on where she has put it and she would be forever weeping over that loss, just one more after all the other things she has lost. But none of this is real. The album is not in the chiffonier, nor is it on her knees. She does not have to go look for it, but neither does she take it everywhere with her; instead, it rests, it lies, it awaits her—that's it—it always waits for her in the little drawing room, Alda's reception room, the only thing that is on top of the piano, and it is open to one page, the page where the snapshot is, since all the other pages are empty, as Aurelia very well knows. The drawing room, the piano, the album, the black page, the white page of some unknown person's album, the portrait of a woman in profile, a woman who was, or would be, or might be Aurelia, her profile standing out against another profile, that one of stone, with a flattened nose as if it had been sliced off by a sword, and below it some words written in sepia ink: "Axel Munthe's house, Anacapri."

Alda is breathing heavily, gasping, she nearly stops breathing, she is going to suffocate. Her throat is a small, retractable orifice, always in danger of closing. And life, an entire life is able to escape through one's throat, it could be imprisoned in the throat, depending on some unpredictable moment during which any other sensation might vanish and the intensity, the desire, the necessity of a decisive effort might collect at that point and blot out everything else. The throat can gradually and slowly get smaller and smaller, and tiny thorns, minute needles will squeeze the small remaining opening more and more tightly together, to obliterate it, to hinder the passage of air absolutely forever. Death comes then. Death is simple. It is always on the verge. The strange thing is that one can remain this way for so long and yet not die. Not finish dying, not take that step, that small, gentle step, surrounded by silence.

Alda.

Alda is breathing.

She is breathing heavily.

She is at the point of suffocating.

Alda touches the little bell hopelessly, a bell of purple and white glass engraved with figures of leaves and flowers, the bell that had not been there in her room before but on the long table in the long dining room surrounded by windows.

Alda looks at the bell but does not make it ring. She touches it, yes, but in order to fondle it, as if it were a frozen flower.

Alda does not have the bell. She has lost it. She put it away a long time ago—many years—inside a drawer full of linen sheets   all   covered   with   tiny   yellowish   spots,   and forgot it.

Alda holds the bell between her hands, her two hands, like a chalice. She gazes at it attentively as if she were wishing to see something else, and then, without realizing it, she lets it fall into the ferns beneath her window, the garden ferns that receive it so gently.

Alda should not do these things. She no longer knows what she is doing. She has no memory. She does not want to remember.

Alda is motionless. Motionless all the time. It is horrible to be this way constantly, without moving. Lying down. Gazing at the ceiling. Without a single movement. Her back is beginning to ache. At first it is easy to localize the pain, to know where it began. Afterward it's not. Afterward the pain is everything and there is nothing else. Not too strong a pain, one that you can bear, one you might almost enjoy, that helps you to go on living.

No. She is not feeling any pain. She is lying down. She does not move. But nothing is hurting her. She feels nothing. Only her tongue, very thick, inside the mouth she cannot open. Enlarged, swollen, but no pain. Her tongue. The mouth she will never be able to open again—perhaps because she is dead? Her lips dry. Teeth clenched, one against the other. Thirst. Infinite, never-ending. The desire to dampen her lips with ice water. The desire to shout for them to bring her water this very minute: a huge pitcher of water, full of ice.

Alda is not on her bed. She has no pain. Feels no thirst. She is not going to suffocate. None of that is real. She is sick, of course, but her illness is something else. If she could only know how Alda became sick so long, so very long ago!

Alda has strange dreams. She dreams without ever having fallen asleep. That's it: she never sleeps. She is always wakeful. Day and night.

And now she is not in her room, she is not sitting in the

corner, in the half-light, waiting for something.

She is looking at a photo album, a thick album with a studded cover the color of lilac, on which little daisies are outlined in gilt, along with the profiles of blonde girls and acanthus leaves. She keeps thumbing through the pages, slowly, one by one, each time making an enormous effort as if her arm were refusing to move, as if it were made of lead. Her arm is heavy, and the old snapshots are heavy as well. Everything is huge—the album, the snapshots, her arm, her hand, the effort she puts into it, her movements. Hundreds of pictures and never the face she seeks, sought for amid the little wicker tables and folding screens, the palm trees and the statues, the mirrors and the roses, always the roses. The album full. Not a single empty space, not a single page free, no page where one might be able to put the image of a woman in profile, all by itself, in the middle, over the face also in profile of a stone head, now almost without any visible features, both of them situated, the woman and the statue, on the edge of a terrace, as if reclining at once on a fragment of sky and a fragment of ocean.

The album Alda is looking at is too full. Full of pictures and without words. Without the five words that might provide a still greater, more definitive firmness to the posture of a moment that should not be forgotten.

Alda is seated among some cushions on a small, gilded sofa in the little drawing room. She never moves from there. Everyone is after her. They all come near. They all wish to speak with her. They are all her friends. They cajole her, flatter her, ask her to tell the story again—for the hundreth time—of the trip around the world, to tell them about Hong Kong and India, about the lengthy crossing, the dances on the huge ocean liner, that strange adventure that took place at Pompeii. She speaks almost in a whisper, with some reluctance, as if not wanting to say too much, sagely more generous with herself than with the story, extending around her words a veiled translucence that she alone is capable of measuring out. Siegfried slowly going up the ancient river amid the mists and the forests hung with mistletoe (she has always known and loved the melancholy of certain heroic, Wagnerian chords). Music stirs her, transports her to a landscape of fog and dampness, of huge pine trees, ancient birches and gothic towers, a landscape through which valiant knights move to their encounters with death, bearing next to their hearts, protected by a heavy breastplate, the petals of a shattered rose. *Riding, riding, riding. Valor has gotten weary, longing is very deep . . .*

The whole palace is vibrating, taken over by an intense, uncontainable happiness. The cut-glass lamps are quivering, the mirrors flanked by the gold columns, the two Titians that are in the great ballroom, the coffered ceilings and the tapestries between the arches overlooking the stairs, with the latter being touched by the quick, excited steps of the people passing through the huge iron door set with glass panels and going on up to the first landing to inspect the upper-floor balcony, contemplating the ones already gathered there, the ones dancing down below, in order to descend afterward by way of the other staircase to the entrance of the small drawing room and the terrace and finally, almost violently, joining in with the euphoria of the party.

Alda gazes at herself. She sees herself in all the mirrors (that seem to her all too few, since she would like to see her image reproduced a thousand times). She dances without stopping. She enjoys herself. She is twenty years old and married now. She has been happy. She loves the music, the talk, and all the people. She goes through the whole house, stopping for a moment in the dining room to caress the purple and white glasses briefly with her gaze, the initials engraved on the dinner service, her own profile reflected in three mirrors at once. She lets her hands run gently over the length of her figure, too thin, scarcely held in by the iridescent chiffon, and her ring, the heavy wedding band that was always too loose, slips off silently to lose itself in the carpet.

All about, the street, the breeze, the darkening afternoon, the city, the ocean surround the mansion like the waves of an inconstant surf that threatens nothing, that merely curls up on the beach with a soothing rhythm. The high stone walls, the covered terrace on the upper floor, the small shutters, too tiny for the high gray walls, all lose their rigidity, become flexible, assimilating themselves to the doughy, dense, tropical nature of the old buildings, their plaster cornices, their stained glass windows, and their immeasurably intricate balconies.

Alda stops beyond the bridge, the ancient, topaz-colored bridge, and takes a brief look at the city above the motley shops of the goldsmiths and the hawking calls of the peddlers. From there on the hill, the city regains the symmetry, the impeccable tidiness it has in the canvases of the primitives.

Florence is glinting in the depths of the valley, almost ancient, uniform, lineal, ochre and gray without nuances of hue, without secrets. And Alda transports it, substitutes it for her seaside city, which is messy, at once both generous and recondite, but always restless, never ceasing to offer the vague, ambiguous risk of danger. She will carry away all that remoteness, that serenity, that guarantee of eternal life, that charm against everything that might be introduced inside the houses to destroy them—the salt, the termites, and anything that gets behind the interior of the beings and bores into them until they become hollow or useless, ready to be collected by death. In this way, the solemn cinquecento residence abandoned the Via della Vigna Nuova forever.

And now the palazzo is here, safe and sound, obstinately, while the rosebushes she has had planted in the garden have taken sick; they have lost their vitality, and they are dying. The palazzo is not touched when a strange, invisible plague begins to devour the bushes' tenderest shoots. There was something wrong from the beginning. Something lacking. Perhaps when the first stone was placed in the middle of the bald patch they first had to clear, to cleanse of so much wild vegetation, almost a jungle, that used to cover the huge enclave, like an unlikely island in the midst of the city. Or perhaps when they began to live in the house without first allowing it to be blessed in order to make it more their own, maybe that was when the spirit that had dwelt within and wanted to be included was wrenched away from it.

Alda is fondling the page of the calendar, sliding her fingers softly over the thick surface of the numbers, going over them affectionately, examining them. The yellowed page has a silky feel, almost velvet-like, and her finger slips along without finding any roughness. AUGUST 20, 1933.

The garden is invading the inner precincts, it ravishes the spaces that used to be forbidden it, coming in from beneath the doors, like damp green moss, a bed of little mushrooms that spring up in the oddest way from one day to the next; it penetrates the empty spaces that had formerly let the air in between the window frames and the wall, in the shape of the twisting, fragile climbing weeds that flood the interior with a sickly, over-sweet, nocturnal fragrance; it slips in timidly through the cracks that have barely begun to open between the ceiling of the lower story and the floor of the one above, and it is beginning to lift the tiles, to make its way violently in among the seams where the cement has already started to crack, in those places where the stucco is coming loose from the wall to leave dark hollows, empty cavities, open to the eye: through all these harsh, dark pathways, these improvised trails, surreptitiously but as if guided by some final end, by a design that will not be put off, the ivy slips in.

And here is where the palazzo ceases to be impregnable. At first the garden had the charm of negligence, of a certain freedom that never went outside the bounds of correction and restraint. Cypresses and palm trees lived together, hydrangeas and crotalaria, poincianas and pine trees. Then the proliferation of climbing roses and ivy, the ferns and the asparagus, all sorts of caladium, amaranthus, and oleanders, all the wild grasses that blocked the walks, the velvety, fleshy leaves that invaded the formerly unobstructed paths—all this restored the garden, which had been shapely, neat, and orderly, to a previous condition, one that used to be in possession of the broad, uncultivated terrain before any humans dwelt there, throughout the whole time it had remained forgotten and enclosed by a thick hedge of thistles and thorns. Except that now it was not a natural disorderliness like that of certain wild but innocent landscapes, uncontaminated as yet by the spirit of mankind. Now the garden began to be inhabited by a soul, began to live in some other way, a life that more and more had to take its nourishment from the life of the palazzo and those who lived within.

Aurelia closes her eyes, trying futilely and silently to go back to the empty date on the calendar, the date that might be a key, the key to everything, but that—hollow and strange—provides no recollection.

She must get up. Go back to her ceaseless wandering around. Go through the whole palazzo once more, from top to bottom. Guarding against entry from outside. Hindering the plants from getting through. Shutting off all holes. The doors and windows. The highest shutters, the ones in the rooms on the top floor that no one ever used, those too. Because if she does not hurry, the curse of the roses will come in through any of those apertures, through any one of them or through them all.

She must be on her guard that the palazzo's soul does not escape, that it does not become dispersed, that it does not disappear as happens with perfumes that are allowed to go free

for too long. The house has been open for too long. In her
negligence she has left it open. She has forgotten to shut the
doors from the inside, to secure the locks, to shoot the bolts, to
put up the thick iron bars where the supports hidden behind the
curtains let one know it is safest to protect the strong, wooden
doors with something more, something that will prevent any
intrusion. But this is not a question of an intruder. Aurelia has
already forgotten, too, that there can be intruders, strangers,
thieves with inexplicable intentions that are capable of getting
inside the dwellings where one lives. She does not fear that. She
fears, she is horrified by, another more dangerous invasion,
that of the spirit that has taken control of the garden, that obliges
the roses to die off and the ivy to grow unrestrainedly and to
work its way inside. She needs to close the doors, the windows,
the gates, the shutters. She needs to get the tables moved, the
heaviest chests of drawers, the high-backed chairs, anything
that will work when placed against a door, anything that will
block passage.

Lucila, Lucila! Where can Lucila be? Why isn't she
coming to help her? Oh, to talk with someone! If Lucila were
to come, she would be able to have someone to talk with. Could
it be that Lucila has abandoned her, too?

Aurelia calls, she shouts, and Lucila's name resounds,
swollen and enormous, without managing to produce an echo,
merely amplified outlandishly by the emptiness.

Lucila is not here. She left, too, oh so many years ago
. . . Everyone gone. They have all left her. She alone must
protect herself.

All by herself she will close up, she is shutting, now
there is little left . . . she will block off all the exits and entrances
and leave no opening. She has always begun with the highest
up. One by one, the windows behind the shutters that were
supposed to keep the dust off the books in the library. Then, one
floor below, the slats of the blinds without glass windows, the

wooden shutters, the jalousies, in each of the rooms reserved
for the guests, for the guests of the guests, acquaintances and
strangers alike. Afterward on the second floor, the ten dining-
room windows scarcely ajar; the four in each bedroom, all shut,
of course, no doubt about that, and nervously inspected from
top to bottom by feverish fingers, more and more difficult to
control. Finally, the large drawing room, the small drawing
room, the ballroom, the windows that open out on the terrace,
the doors that can be opened onto the tiny garden within, that
has no exit to the street. The door that closes off Alda's room,
the room where those other doors are, the only ones that offer
access to the interior garden, the one without an exit to the
street. The garden she always loved. The garden that was never
hers. The garden where all the roses were, are, should be.

Docilely the door yields, with no resistance. The room
smells of tepid dampness and flowers confined, the same smell
as in church, in caves. She submerges herself voluptuously in
the verdure of the ferns everywhere overflowing the mirror's
frame in the muddled light, in a strange peace, deep and
timeless. And there she remains, staring fixedly at the mirror.
Gazing at herself, seeing Alda's image, her own image, the
face that was lost and, finally, with difficulty won back. The
eyelids close, overwhelmed by a strange, prolonged, nebulous
fatigue, and then, softly, something abandons her forever.

II

The
*H*ouse

*T*hey have just put the cradle in the same corner as always. The cradle made of white iron, lined with lace, with a tulle mosquito netting. They walk from one side of the room to the other. I do not move. They are talking about the new baby.

"Have you noticed the resemblance . . . ? He's the spitting image. If it had been a girl . . ."

Everyone comes closer. It is the women who carefully part the net. Prince, who is an Irish setter then, approaches too. He puts up his two front paws and sticks his nose in. They push him away, tell him to leave. But there he stays, beneath the cradle, stretched out with one of his front paws sweetly tucked under the other and his nose completely flat on the floor. He remains there, stretched out beneath the cradle. How many years has Prince been lying under the cradle, guarding the new baby? I, who have been watching all this time, cannot remember.

Now Prince is sitting on the wicker sofa, between Consuelo on one side, and a young American who might be named Jim. Consuelo is dressed in black and has an enormous hat on with long ostrich feathers. She barely smiles. She is wearing her glasses lightly perched on the bridge of her nose: oval-shaped glasses, the lenses surrounded by a fine band of gold. Consuelo smiles like a Leonardo archangel, with a vague, faraway ambiguity. On Prince's other side, Jim, with a self-assured gaze and no expression on his face, looks straight ahead from behind his glasses that are designed to correct nearsightedness. His wavy hair has been parted in the middle. On his lap, a straw hat. Neither Consuelo nor Jim needs to speak.

At a certain point, Prince has jumped down from his place on the yellow sofa. Then he has taken off at a run, leaving betweeen Consuelo and Jim a void that could only be filled with words. And neither one is willing to say them.

At the back of the room, the folding screen situated in a place right where the sun shines in with excessive intensity. So much so that the screen floats surrounded by a halo, levitating in the somewhat heavy air of three in the afternoon. This screen is fairly new. Consuelo's father has had it placed there recently. And already it seems definitive, rooted there forever. Albertina, twelve years old, places herself near the screen holding a fan she begins to move too slowly, with an absent-minded gesture. When she stops fanning herself, she is eighteen, and no longer looks distractedly at the oversized majolica vase, but fixes her gaze on an imprecise point situated—perhaps one could say—in infinite space. Prince is nowhere to be seen, neither at that moment nor any other.

Prince is sitting at the feet of Consuelo (the mother), who in turn is seated in a rocking chair by the balcony. Consuelo rocks unhurriedly, sure that she may continue doing so for as long as she wants; that she may, if she so wishes, never stop, because there is nothing in the world more important to do—nor, perhaps, will there ever be from then on. Then with a sudden decisiveness she leans down to pick up Prince, who is a small Pomeranian, and rock him interminably on her lap. Next she begins to speak to him in a low voice, as if she needed to tell him a secret.

Everything around me is new. The breeze reaches us day and night, because the windows are never shut. I settled in here two days ago, when the last workman left. I am this place. I am this place, and I am located here, both at the same time. I constantly look out from the windows, the balconies, the terrace, to get a glimpse of the sea. We are just a few steps from the sea. Between us and the sea lies only the street, the *malecón**, and the raised wall on which children sometimes walk, parents holding them by the hand. The upstairs terrace has many columns. That is where I love to be. It is the area of the house I most prefer. The terrace has a roof, but no windows. Only columns, and between them, unceasingly, the sea breezes.

When will I see you? You haven't even walked by on the *malecón* like you have at other times. I've stopped counting the days since I last saw you. Why, sometimes, do you stop loving me like this? Every day I position myself behind the louvered shutters. I love you so much! I spend whole hours remembering the color of your skin, and your eyes, and your hair. I can't go on living without having you. One of these days perhaps I will die. Will you come this afternoon? Yes, I mustn't doubt it. That way, at least I'll have all day long to hope and wait. I will wait for you, then I'll go on waiting through the

---

*Translator's note: *malecón*: Havana's seawall boulevard, initially constructed in 1901 and lined with large houses built in the grand style. During winter months when strong winds blow from the north and waves crash over the embankment, parts of the *malecón* are closed to traffic.

afternoon, from behind the shutters. Don't fail me. Don't leave me waiting yet another time, until night falls and there is no longer any doubt that you won't be coming. Love, my love . . . !

Meanwhile, she busies herself arranging flowers. She doesn't know how to do anything else. Not even sew. Or embroider. Or play the piano. How could she not have learned all that in school, when her sister . . . ? She keeps an eye on the flowers, changing them as soon as they begin to wilt; it is a mania, she cannot stand for them to wilt. Or perhaps she keeps changing the flowers simply because she doesn't know how to do anything else.

It is her uncle, or her father, who is reading on the terrace, seated in a woven rocker. The breeze is too strong and it turns the pages of his book. So then he secures them with a small marker made of gold metal, painstakingly worked with leaves and flowers in enamel. While he reads, he absentmindedly caresses the enameled setting with the ball of his thumb. Albertina comes up without making a sound and reads over his shoulder. " . . . I am totally convinced that the common opinion of naturalists is correct, that is, that they are all related to the wild dove (*Colomba livia*) . . ." The breeze is too strong and it blows Albertina's dress and hair around.

With a leap Prince gets up on the chair, woven into patterns of spirals and circles. Since then he has not gotten down again. But he is not the same Prince that lay down underneath the cradle. He is the other one. And there is yet another. This one, the third one—or perhaps the first—is leaning against the gilded cage, trying to catch the little bird as if he, Prince, were a cat. Actually he is a diminutive black Pekinese. Julio, Albertina's father, Consuelo's father, husband of Consuelo (the mother)—long before any of those three relationships exists—attacks Prince with a small stick, a flexible little rod they have just given him as a present. Then he inserts the rod into the cage and moves it from side to side, until he drives the bird crazy, as it keeps flying around trying to find somewhere to perch. This scene lasts only for about two minutes because the bird collapses, exhausted, before the boy or the dog get tired. All of this happens here, in this room, the one where the cradle also is, and Prince the Irish setter, who keeps watch.

"What could those memories have been that were torturing you one October afternoon eleven years ago?" The hand that writes this at this moment, my hand, is only repeating something that another hand is writing at a moment exactly the same as this one, prolonged until now, on a gray, melancholy afternoon on a Sunday, October 16, 1927. Another hand, holding not a fountain pen, but a long-handled pen that has to be dipped constantly into a white, yellow and blue porcelain inkwell, a very large inkwell with a tiny, round receptacle on top filled to the brim with sepia-colored ink. The two hands, the two dates, August 28, 1967 and October 16, 1927, blur into a present that, from now on, will not disappear again.

Everything around me—and I myself, who form part of this second-floor window of polished glass from where one can make out the entire house, almost—is slightly less new. Sometimes dust settles for many long days on some of us and no one bothers to remove it. I've heard it said that the house has deteriorated a little. And so it has, perhaps, if they say so.

The sofa where Consuelo (the daughter), Jim, and Prince or Prince, Jim, and Consuelo are sitting—because the order can be reversed if desired—suddenly disappears, without my having noticed when this happened, has happened or is happening. In its place is a large chair upholstered in flowered cretonne, empty—and then (it is difficult to say "then," or to think it, because everything is occurring at the same time) the same large chair is occupied by Consuelo (the mother), dressed in a long, heavily starched white robe that covers her down to her feet. A ray of sun, entering through one of the balconies facing the *malecón*, illuminates only Consuelo's forehead, her not yet completely gray hair parted down the middle, and the legs of the marble statue of an Italian peasant girl placed atop a column. The statue is behind Consuelo, a bit to her left. I couldn't say if this happened before, or after, the moment when Jim, Prince, and Consuelo (the daughter) were together on the sofa, in the same place in the living room. This is the first time my memory fails me.

Albertina, pregnant, reclines amid the pillows of the *chaise longue*, wrapped in a warm bathrobe of velvety white plush. It is cold. No one knows—she does not know—why they leave the windows open in the middle of winter. They should remember that the sea is very close, and that at this time of day it is windy, it is always windy. But she cannot get up to go shut them. Now she is very tired. This is normal. Prince, the Pomeranian, comes over and licks her bare feet. Then she realizes why she was cold.

"Has he called you again on the telephone? I told you already I don't like him. If your father were alive . . . or your brothers . . . You should be more careful. He's a stranger."
"Someday I'm going to marry him."

She is no longer there in that window, watching the sea; she is looking out another window where you can also contemplate the Atlantic, but now from her house in New York. Behind her, in the bed, her father lies dead. Her father has died of pneumonia in New York. She accompanies the body in a cargo and passenger ship that slowly heads down toward the Gulf. The ship makes calls at almost all the Atlantic Coast ports. From the deck, she (who could be Albertina or Consuelo, because in this circumstance they are interchangeable) spends hours looking toward land, just as before—here in this window and back there in the house in New York—she looked toward the sea. While she rests on deck, covered up to her shoulders with a Scottish blanket the first officer has brought especially for her, she remembers things that happened when she was a little girl and was never apart from her father. But she remembers only sluggishly, for both she and her memories are wrapped in a gelatinous, dense substance, like the one that envelops dreams.

Julio, his two sons and his two daughters come every day to see the house, now that it is almost finished. He is glad to have decided it was worth making a slight effort to buy such a well-situated lot by the sea. Every day his children will see the ships coming and going. That way, they will want to know other lands, to travel, not to stay anchored forever like him in Havana. Until now he has spent his life dreaming of the trip he will make to New York. Meanwhile, he has resigned himself to looking through the catalogues of import houses (he is a customs supervisor) and twice a year ordering the most beautiful objects offered by representatives of the most prestigious companies of Paris and New York.

My fear of losing you is infinite. I'm jealous. Fierce feelings of jealousy eat me up inside. Jealous of all the desires you may have had. Jealous of those you might still have. When will we be together for good? Today you mentioned something a woman once said to you, and it implied an intimacy of the kind you and I still have not been able to enjoy. I would like to penetrate into the deepest part of your being, to convince myself that there, inside, I am the only one who matters in your life. And that you are mine, and mine alone.

We have never had a garden. Only a few flowers up on the flat roof. She was the one who wanted to make an arbor out of vines, thinking how much he would like it, but perhaps the sea air affected it badly. It never took well, and later on her mother came and planted jasmine. With the jasmine, what happened was that the breeze almost always blew away its perfume. But no one dared pull it out. A plant like that, so fragile, so intimate, cannot be touched again once it has been planted. She, who spends so much time arranging flowers inside the house, has never again thought about the small garden on the roof.

Consuelo has just sat down at the piano for the first time in so long. Music cannot be played while in mourning. "I never would have thought he would leave us so soon." "I want you to convey to your mother, Albertina, your brothers, the pain I feel along with you." "My former world is so far away! I have received a hard blow with this news." "Please believe that from the bottom of my soul I share the grief that has stunned all of you." Czerny exercises, after all, are not music. It is the same thing as practicing a lesson; no one could criticize her for it. But first she caresses the piano and remembers the day when, during a hurricane, the windows burst open tumultuously from the force of the wind, the rain came in, and the piano, full of water and covered with leaves carted in by the storm, ended up in a corner of the hall, crushing the marble statue of a young Italian peasant girl as it rammed into her. The scales, with no transition, slide into a more complex harmony, and suddenly the house is inundated with the sonorous melodies of Beethoven.

Prince, up on the lap of Consuelo (the mother), sitting on the sofa between Jim and Consuelo (the daughter), licking the bare feet of Albertina (the daughter), five months pregnant and reclining on the *chaise longue* in the hall, is a black Pomeranian, so black that it is difficult to make out his eyes in the midst of all the hair around them. Prince, on guard beneath the cradle, being petted by Albertina (the daughter), who is also pregnant, supporting her hand on his left front paw while she pets him, is a red setter with a smooth, shiny coat and big eyes the color of dark amber, at the same time tender and far away. When Prince is up on the sofa, he has a kind of cruel look in his eyes. When Prince lets Albertina (the daughter) pet him he has a look that might be called melancholy, if he were not a dog.

The new baby is several months old now, and she is a girl. Consuelo (the mother) holds her while she rests, seated with her back to the gold-framed mirror where all the light coming in through the balcony is dazzling. For a moment when the movement of the waves is very strong, the mirror captures it, and the living room (situated on the first floor) oscillates briefly in the middle of sea, at the same level as the ship on the horizon beginning its entry into the bay.

Consuelo (the daughter) and Consuelo (the mother) appear for an instant at a second-floor window, looking out at the sea, surrounded by the window frame as if there were someone outside ready to take their photograph. Consuelo (the mother), standing forward, is still young, dressed in black and white with a tight bodice, resting a closed fan on the window ledge; Consuelo (the daughter), is to her left and slightly behind, in such a way that she can put her (right) arm around Consuelo's (the mother's) shoulders while leaning a bit against her left shoulder, with her left hand lightly touching the left arm of Consuelo (the mother). The daughter is dressed in white and has her hair tied back with a ribbon of the same color. Both contemplate the sea.

I think about those postcards I waited for so anxiously day after day and that filled me with emotion. You, between bronze lions in a park in New York. You, with your felt hat in your hand, in that same park, but now next to a tree completely bare of leaves. You, leaning on the rail of the ship, waving goodbye to me. You, climbing the three steps of the boarding house where you live (used to live) in Brooklyn. And sometimes the other postcards, with too-delicate colors, postcards with roses, lilies, hydrangeas, spikenards. All of them dated in the same place, between February and November of 1918.

There are empty lapses. Shorter or longer periods during which the living room is empty, and also the dining room, the rooms on the upper two stories, the terrace, and the small garden on the roof. As hard as I try to fill them, or at least to recall some memory, a living image, the anticipation of something not yet taken place, a contact, a desire, someone's dream, stray words of an interrupted dialogue, a silhouette behind the polished glass panes—as hard as I try to concentrate on the traces that must have been left, I cannot discover even the slightest sign. Everything stays mute. And then I, who form part of this window from where one can make out the entire house, am incapable of awakening something I imagine must be there, palpitating on the margins of things, as if held inside a hollow tuning fork. Sometimes when this happens, the chair woven into an excess of spirals, into a baroque lace of circles and movement, begins to stand out in solitary splendor, apart from everything else. All the other objects disappear and the chair is left, in that place in the living room where Albertina, at twelve years of age, sits fanning herself for a period of time indefinitely prolonged.

But now Albertina is not present. Not present either, there at the back of the living room, almost within the luminosity penetrating inside from the patio, is that tall woman whose name I have forgotten, if I ever knew it (someone who left no memories, someone whom the house has forgotten). Only the chair is there, almost majestic, alive, pulling away from the fragile matter out of which a serene permanence is made, an indestructible certainty. Only the chair is left.

The room has grown dark. The nun, seated in a high-back chair that is too stiff and straight, is reading a thick missal, or perhaps the Imitation of Christ. The others have gone to bed. In the room there is an intense smell of medicine, of alcohol, of old things, of concentrated dampness. The nun gets up, goes over to the bed, and sits down again, approximately every fifteen minutes. At that hour of the early morning there are no sounds to be heard, just every now and then the bell of a passing streetcar whirling light into the room as it goes by, after which everything becomes dark again. The nun reads by the light of a small green glass lamp. She gets up and goes over to the bed again, with the same indifferent manner, like someone carrying out a mechanical job with imperturbable precision. This time Consuelo (the mother) has stopped breathing. The nun takes the intravenous needle out of her bone-thin arm. Then she takes a small mirror from the dresser and holds it over Consuelo's lips, although she knows this is useless. Immediately she puts a white handkerchief pulled from her pocket onto the emaciated face, and lightly presses shut the partially-open eyelids. Only after she has done all this does she take down the crucifix that was hanging over the headboard and put it between Consuelo's hands, which she has first carefully placed one over the other. Then she goes to wake them up.

Albertina, at eighteen, pulls away from the place

where she was fanning herself and sits on the marble top of a console table, clutching a scattered bouquet of roses. Then, her back to the mirror, she holds only one rose in her right hand, the one corresponding to the arm she rests on the staircase railing. The mirror duplicates the crystal chandelier and the excessive brilliance coming in from the balcony. She closes her eyes a little to avoid being blinded by the light.

Prince, the Pomeranian, runs around the house as if he didn't know where he was. Changes have been made. They have taken away some pieces of furniture and brought in others. And in addition, because of an extravagant whim of Julio's (opposed in vain by the mother Consuelo who is so austere), a room that will be his is being built on the top floor. A place where he can go as a refuge, that from outside will be seen as an enclosed gallery jutting out from the façade, and that above all will be noticed because it breaks up the unencumbered harmony the façade had until now—crowned simply by the terrace colonnade—into ripples of carved borders, garlands, and edges, into a vegetal profusion that overwhelms the upper part of the three gallery windows and extends to the ironwork of their little balconies and to their glass panes, colored and white, decorated with fleurs-de-lys and the leaves of fantastic plants. Julio wanted to add a French detail to the house; once again, he wanted to console himself for not being able to travel to Europe. Now the house has its Art Nouveau gallery. The sunflowered window panes tint the violence of the light that acquires an orangish glimmer inside when the windows are closed. The objects already have started arriving, milk glass vases in blue, green, red, orange, enameled table lamps, sphinxes inlaid with mother-of-pearl, plates to hang on the walls painted with irises and hydrangeas and with languid-eyed women's faces, framed by long vegetal locks. Prince has found his spot: a chair with dragon-fly shaped arms that seems to have been made for just such a tiny creature. It is likely that this will be his permanent place. The gallery, of course, has been built on the northern façade, facing the sea. Julio likes to stay there for hours, doing nothing, contemplating his treasures, especially when a strong wind is blowing outside and the sea is churning, when the waves leap over the sea wall, wetting the street and even spattering the ground-floor portico. It is then, inside that profuse, somewhat delirious atmosphere where all voids have been filled to the brim, that he imagines himself to be in the stern of a sumptuous ship, heading towards the unknown. It is now 1907.

This morning I woke up feeling anxious. I had just had a very strange dream. A dream in which you, my love, were marrying my sister and then going away alone on a trip, a long trip from which you would never return. I got up exhausted, as if I had been walking all night without stopping. This happens to me often. I dream, dream without stopping and wake up fatigued, worn out, empty inside, just as if the sap had been drawn all out of me, as if I were a plant no one bothered to water or take care of, abandoned in the darkest part of the garden. How silly I'm being! It's your fault, it's you who makes me feel this way, and it's because of you, because of your fickleness and the temperamental way you are, that I dream these things. My dear little boy, don't you ever pause to think about the way you're hurting me?

Consuelo takes down books from the shelves one by one, cleans them off and leafs through them lazily with no desire to read, just to take in effortlessly the stimulus of a phrase to savor slowly that afternoon when she goes to the concert, where she can fantasize, imagine, that all the melodies she hears are merely the development into infinity of that small phrase, found at random in a book about Bruges, the dead city, with drawings by a Spanish illustrator.

Once again, another of those lapses where everything stays silent. The lights, both the sunlight and the lamplight, fade out, and the surfaces of things, where memories remain locked up, become opaque. How long will it go on this time? That is difficult to know, because in reality nothing is happening any longer within a kind of time where events follow one after another, where there is a past, a present and a future. Everything is happening now, in an unlimited now, where what was the past and what could have been the future vanish. Everything evens out, carries the same weight of existence, happens at the same time and never stops happening. For it has never ceased to be a possibility, and all words and things have found their place again in something called always. But the danger is that suddenly this always (assuming the possibility that something might come about suddenly exists within the inescapable reality that things happen always) will turn, definitively, into an absolute nonexistence of time. A danger always lying in wait.

The calendars mark, at the same time, the following dates: September 21, 1929; March 25, 1955; December 2, 1964; October 10, 1916; October 31, 1930. A strange phenomenon that probably will not be repeated.

All the outer walls facing the sea now appear to be invaded by a fungus, or a malignant rash. First the paint cracked, and then it fell off in some places along with the plaster, both softened by the humidity. The columns of the portico and the upper terrace, the stone parts of the façade, show small holes opened up by the constant spray of the sea. For although the waves have never come up far enough to bathe the façade, the salt-heavy air ceaselessly deposits drops that pull away from the surf jumping over the retaining wall, the sea wall that separates the street from the rocks and the sea. The peculiar smell of the sea, brought in by the breeze or the wind, has taken possession of the interior of the house, which more and more has the character of an absurd ship careened on the ocean shore. The house is no longer the house but an enclosure made for the sea, impregnated by its marine smell, taste, consistency. A mossy green now peeks out from between the bricks uncovered by its corrosive, penetrating motion.

Albertina and Consuelo, standing by the console table and the mirror, speaking in low voices, go back vertiginously to a similar moment lived twenty years before when they were five and six years old, respectively. Albertina, with her short hair full of curls; Consuelo, with very long hair almost down to her waist, straight and tied back with a white ribbon. They are passing seashells back and forth to each other, seashells which are almost all broken; stones; pieces of rough wood and smooth glass, their cutting edges now removed; snails; coiled and hardened worms, preserved like fossils without decay; pressed leaves that resemble fish skeletons, their veins like bones; a seahorse; pieces of sponge; pebbles. They divide everything up silently, without arguing. Twenty years later in the same place, Consuelo—saying something in a low voice—gives Albertina a sealed envelope that Albertina hides inside the book she is holding, because at that moment Consuelo (the mother) approaches. During this entire scene, both Albertina and Consuelo have the feeling that they are repeating something they have lived through before.

Albertina sits at the open desk full of little drawers and compartments and picks out from among several notebooks a black one, an oblong rectangle covered in Russian leather. She opens it to the second page and inscribes there: "Eleven years, how life goes by . . ." She writes in the elegant, slender, straight hand that is part of her identity. It pleases her to write with an exaggerated perfectionism, as if that way she were leaving an eternal, inerasable trace. "The monotonous sound of the rain, hitting the tiles of the passageway, keeps reaching my ears. There is a sticky humidity in the air and only the night permits . . ." All the rest is ellipsis.

The good thing is that now time has ceased to pass, and from now on (which will never cease being now) everything will be identical to itself. The moment she first took up the pen to write in the black, leather-covered album has remained suspended, latent and at the same time filled to the brim; filled up with all that it is in itself, with all that might have been, with an infinity of possibilities that will never be realized, and that, for the same reason, will be present forever while memory exists and—although this is not so evident—even afterwards as well. And just as that gesture has remained suspended in a deferral that only waits for the beginning of another identical gesture to be redeemed, reproduced, and forever fixed, all other planned and completed gestures, projected and accomplished movements, words both spoken and thought about, dialogues, goals, desires, and dreams also have remained in a latent state.

Julio has ordered everything repaired; the painters, bricklayers, carpenters and blacksmiths have returned. The house is looking like new. In this window one of the panes was broken, and they have already replaced it. It is the one just next to me, and an intense cold has been coming in through that hole since the first days of January, when the north wind started. Now that the little girl is living in the house, sometimes she used to come over, pull up a stool, and stick her hand through the pane in the glass. Then she would start to shout that it was raining, or it was cold, or that the waves were spattering up there. She liked to leave her hand outside for a long time, until it was totally wet. Now she cannot do it anymore because they have put the glass back. Ever since they started repairing the house, everyone walks around in bewilderment, from one end of it to the other, as if they didn't understand what was going on. Only Julio seems to walk with a sure step: he gives orders, stands up on chairs to point out details, takes down paintings to get them new frames, changes the placement of the furniture, the decorations, the family photographs. However, he doesn't allow them to touch a thing in the enclosed gallery, nor has he wanted to rearrange things there. What will they do now with everything that has been moved around, that used to be silent, tranquil, peaceful? With everything that used to be asleep and now is agitated and restless, as if someone had profaned the place where the remains of long-dead relatives were being kept? I do not know if they realize it, but I can feel it, I perceive around me a disquieting itchiness of buried life that has suddenly been brought to the surface, violently demanding a release, a way out. As if the souls of people and things had been waiting for this moment in a prolonged purgatory, now impulsively and imprudently opened up, to be flung to the four winds. Why has Julio done it? Perhaps because he has always lived like this, as if he were floating above everything, with a kind of irresponsibility, with excessive gaiety, forgetting that the world is full of sadness and serious matters. I only know that if this goes on, if no one comes to put a limit on this avalanche of unbound emotions, something sinister is going to happen, something disastrous: the feelings stored away in the corners, the lethargic words, will throw themselves at the walls, will open up cracks in the floor and ceiling, will bring on an explosion just as when a covered pot is put under enormous pressure, and the house will collapse on us and on them, the living and the dead.

This month is as gray and rainy as that other one was thirteen years ago when we met . . . The water has an odious effect on me: it makes me succumb to sleepiness. Thirteen years ago you gave me the bracelet I still wear around my ankle. And nevertheless . . . I'm growing sick from nostalgia, from desire. That infinite vertigo I feel upon seeing myself in your eyes! How long will the torment of living apart from you go on? Everything would be so different if you wanted it to be, if you decided to put an end to this waiting that is so sad, so cruel. You know that you are my only reason for living and despite that . . . Today, since it was the anniversary of the day we met, just to celebrate, I don't know why, maybe so I could leave you the memory before getting too old, I went to the photographer's studio and had several pictures taken of myself. I'm so afraid! Afraid that all of what I'm feeling now might be extinguished, that my body will lose its flexibility, that my eyes will no longer overflow with passion, that my gaze will be extinguished . . . The photographer had me pose several times, always with roses in my hands; standing up, slightly in profile, with a rose in my right hand; facing straight forward, holding two roses, this time in my left hand; sitting on a marble-topped table, clutching a scattered bouquet of roses in my arms. Other roses, many more, had been placed with studied neglect on top of the marble. He promised he would have the pictures ready in three days. You already know they are for you, all for you.

The Italian peasant girl has disappeared from her pedestal, and it is impossible to locate Prince the Pomeranian, Prince the Pekinese or Prince the Irish setter—without forgetting that the three of them are one and the same—in any of the places where they ought to be. The cradle has disappeared too, and the wicker sofa, and the large chair upholstered in flowered linen, and the *chaise longue* that was placed next to the stairs.

Clearly this is why it is impossible to find the dog (the dogs) anywhere. But the chair with the woven spirals has not disappeared, and yet it is not there either. Could it be possible that they are completely gone, for good? I do not think so, and will keep searching.

How long will the summer last? I long for the north winds, I want the wind to go wild and penetrate everywhere, for it to blow the shutters wide open and make the chandeliers swing, so that I can hear the noise the crystals make when they knock against each other. Everything becomes so listless when it is sunny for entire days, one after the other without stopping! Now I realize that those lapses when everything is dead and silent, sunken into a profound lethargy, always occur in the summer. The humidity and the wind are necessary for things to go on living. And for themselves, too.

It is strange that the cradle (which had been lost), the chair woven in spirals now painted white, and the open casket where she lies with a rosary made of seeds from the Mount of Olives twined in her hands, all meet in the same place. Probably because of that strange coincidence, Prince the Irish setter has come back to lie down beneath it, reappearing after such a long time. I make an effort to see, because the atmosphere is clouded and visibility is erratic. The interior of the house and everyone gathered for this reason vanish or rather dissipate, as if they were only there in a dream. I think I can make out from here that they are all praying, women and men. Someone, however, has remained standing next to the coffin for the entire time and now, an instant before they come to close it, has let fall a scattered bouquet of intensely red roses inside. Then, finally, the scene darkens.

From time to time, small corners light up again, there

are flashes that briefly reveal a forgotten gesture, voices, slight shudders. The house has been empty for too long.

Translated by
Kathleen Ross

The
City

*T*he city endures a deferral without limit. No one knows what is going to happen later on. But for the moment each thing participates in the nature of its opposite: everything is what it is and what it is not at the same time. In this way it manages, through an unusual bit of chance, to suspend the passage of time and tighten itself around a compact, solid nucleus that gradually expands more and more until it embraces the entire city. After that precise moment, which has not been created artificially, the city will reject everything that denies, impugns, resists, or places in doubt the duality that is from then on the essence of its nature.

The city is nothing more than its secret places. Enclosed places, spots that are held back from outside glances, everything that is withdrawn or secluded, everything that takes the path of a predestined involution toward an origin that is primitive and intact: hallways and patios and backyards, each one a more intimate stage on the way to the mystery. All of this is suspended amid the rest, floating amid the loquacity, rescued from a dense profusion of futile words.

The streets are empty. Doorways, sidewalks are empty. It is possible that this silence will prevail in the end and eradicate for good the street vendors' cries that until yesterday were still heard sometimes when the wind was favorable. Now a chilly breeze from the north passes through the streets that begin at the edge of the sea and are quickly lost among the inner alleys of the city. Shutters, doors close suddenly. Some of them flap to and fro repeatedly, open and close again in the progression of a rhythm that even as it started up has already registered its silences and pauses.

> *"Havana in 1782 was wretched little village, with more houses built with boards and tile than of stone, and many more built with earthen bricks and mud than of boards." "Going out through the Land Gate, one would get into vegetable plots and farms, with large wooded areas and also huge packs of dogs . . ."*
> *". . . small dwellings of reddish tiles and a single floor. . . Those among them that made the best impression were the ones on the first block of Compostela Street. They were all the same size, more or less, with a single window and a door, the latter made of cedar, using nails with large heads, the former painted in a brick color; all of them with a short flight of stairs and railings made of rough-hewn wood. The streetbed was to be found in its primitive, natural state, full of rocks and without sidewalks."*

Some people are working their way along the streets, searching for their names. Everyone's names have been lost suddenly and they have stopped greeting each other. For some this is a relief. They are starting to enjoy their anonymity; they are searching eagerly in the others' faces because in losing their names they have lost themselves and they fear this loss may be final. As a last, desperate resort they display personal objects, especially their watches, voluptuously pulled from their empty pockets. The watches are the last sign.

Strangely, now that life in some of its manifestations is disappearing, the nature of the city is beginning to solidify around a lasting image, summoned to persist. If anything were to be added after this, that something would not form part of the now stable image; it would keep to one side, futilely, without helping to form anything at all. Assuming that someone might still be able to do so, this would invite some reflection concerning the essence of things—if indeed such a thing exists.

The image: an impasto of pastel colors and whites, with a violent predominance of dirty yellow, rather a cream color, hues blended in a prism of light infinitely broken up, amid cupolas that are gilded and cupolas that are white, and a scattered batch of gothic spires. Further down, friezes and entablatures of all the classical orders, deceitfully supported by columns with rotting surfaces, eaten away by a hundred-year-old illness that sticks to them in order to despoil them. Sick columns as described by Carpentier, sick among words that attempt to bring the shattered image together, the dispersed, ruined nature of the city that does not recognize and never ceases to deny itself. The stifling, obsessive repetition of columns in a landscape that oppressively closes down on them without allowing the city the open ampleness of the blue spaces, the transparency of the Mediterranean. Although the city also has its villas, its white villas floating amid the brilliant green of the gardens, hanging from streets that slip down almost majestically toward the sea. And this is the Mediterranean side of the image.

"In less than three months the epidemic swept the city of Havana clean of a third part of its citizenry. Seven

gravediggers deceased and no one put up for the office. With bodies unable to be accommodated in the Espada cemetery, one was improvised at the Molinos's country home. A huge trench was opened up bordering what is now the Ayesterán Road, and many, not yet deceased, were buried in quicklime."

When threatened, the city takes refuge behind its walls and is unfamiliar with what surrounds it. There, sheltered within its original precinct, it purges itself of all that has been added to it and concentrates on that which was and is its nucleus: its zig-zagging streets, shaded plazas, churches, and also its forts that look toward the sea. Near the docks the smells of tar, hides, salted meats, and brown sugar are sensed once more and, in a coincidence that has nothing strange about it, are fused with the risk of hurricanes that lie in wait during this month of October, together with the always present threat of being attacked. The wall has been raised invisibly, rediscovering its course through entire apartment blocks of recent construction in such a way that in the same group of inhabited housing one part belongs to the walled enclosure and another remains outside it, defenseless. A situation only dimly perceived by its residents.

"In those times during which the mother country believed that the science of governing the colonies was encompassed in the setting up of a few batteries of cannons, they got the idea of building Havana's walls, a work that began at the start of the seventeenth century and was finished toward the end of the eighteenth. Said walls were part of a vast, total fortification, directed as much toward the surrounding countryside as toward the sea or the port; they lacked neither the four gates leading to the suburban areas,

nor posterns leading to the water, drawbridges, a moat both deep and wide, earthworks, magazines, palisades, loopholes, nor crenellated battlements. Thus the most populous city on the island was in fact converted into an immense fortress."

Although neither the residents nor the city itself have memories. The houses too reject memory, they refuse to listen to the voices. They scarcely notice the traces of earlier times residing within; they cover them over and force them into oblivion. The city prefers oblivion and shields itself behind it in order to protect itself from something that—if memory existed—might erode it in secret, underground ways. But there is also another city. A city that is nothing but memory, anchored and forever equal to itself, beside the still waters, themselves motionless, incapable ever of managing to become any of the other cities that it might have been at the beginning—though it is difficult to imagine a beginning for it, as it also is to imagine an end to it, whether soon or late. This city is here forever. It is a city without a before or an after.

Now the city lacks vegetation. It spreads out, gray upon gray, toward marginal, sullen streets. It is the rainless city, abandoned to its condition of brick and mud, its hundred years of dust. The sky descends and, in a compact, filthy cloud, weighs down upon the low roofs, resigned forever to that tiresome proximity to the earth. It never rains. Sometimes an obsessive, impoverished mist falls which worsens the gloom instead of dissipating it. The inhabitants can walk a long time without encountering a tree, and when someone does discover one, then it seems like a ragged silhouette ready to fall apart, to turn into something else, to deny its condition. In this city, the wall that surrounded it completely at one time has disappeared and left the now shapeless enclosure defenceless, reduced to its precarious alleys. The sea does not exist, despite the stubbornness of the residents who insist on referring to its presence and even gather on its gray beaches enclosed by sparse, barren hillocks, mounds of gray dust, beaches of gray sands, a gray sea: a monotonous desolation.

> *". . . when only the five original gates existed, the three in the center, named the Monserrat Gate, the Wall Gate, and the Land Gate, were for public use in carriages, on horseback, and on foot, and the two at the outer extremes, denominated the Point Gate and the Power Gate, were destined especially for trade."*

These are the images superimposed: the city next to the sea and facing the sea; the city with its back to the sea; the city beside the motionless river (as has been said already). The three are one, now and always. And the other one, too: the city without a sea, not even in order to deny it; the riverless city, city without water in any of its manifestations, except rain; the city of stone upon stone, always identical to its origins. All of these are the city. None is *my city*. All of them nullify me.

There is something sinister prowling around it. That something becomes scattered imperceptibly without managing to toughen, or to become anything but a vague announcement about what might happen. It goes around in the city's environs without being able to turn itself into an actual threat. Being impalpable, it lacks material form, is nothing but a single dark, latent possibility of coming into being. At certain hours, that are not always the same ones, it rises to the surface like a slight tremor within solid things, a reverberation in the light, a movement upon the face of stagnant waters. Then it disappears. The people who perceive it keep that dark knowledge to themselves, not without shivering slightly, fearful of having anticipated the repetition of something that should have happened already. And it goes no further.

Those who have always resided in the city do not recognize it. No longer is it their city but that of others, the unknown ones, those who have been turned unexpectedly into its only survivors. Innocent survivors of a disaster they did not even have to witness. Survivors with memories, with the alien, indifferent curiosity of travelers who walk quickly and suddenly are horror-struck to be faced with one long, useless day too many in a city that doesn't recognize them, that rejects them.

"The white women, at least those who were not wending their ways to church, used to ride in two-wheeled buggies, which were just beginning to become common then and to take the place of the volantes and calèches that had been in use since the end of the last century. They were nearly always occupied by three women seated facing forward in the carriage's single seat, the older ones on the outside, leaning softly back, and the youngest one in the middle, always erect, because neither these buggies nor our volantes were really built for three people, but for two. Though it was after nine o'clock in the morning, the sun would not have not warmed up too much, as the season was so far advanced; therefore, nearly all the buggies had their tops down, revealing in all their glory the lovely faces of, for the most part, young women, dressed in white or else in light colors, with neither head scarves nor bonnets, the black plaits of their locks held tight with a tortoise shell comb, called a 'peineta de teja,' and their shoulders and arms uncovered."

For a moment, perhaps only this spring, the streets have been populated with trees and the parks with a wet, downy verdure. Everything is full of blue and yellow, a blue that sometimes prefers to be lilac-colored, and a deep, Roman or Florentine yellow. Whole blocks are now covered with parks, with gentle slopes, lakes, and weeping willows. The parks are in the English style, not too severe, made to preserve forever the appearance of spontaneity, of nature untamed, and now and then they surreptitiously turn into Italian parks—a little wild. To start with, the city doubtless was made for the English parks, the gardens clotted with hydrangeas and willows, with a measure of romanticism and a dash of melancholy, a tolerable melancholy. Thus too were the greens alongside the river, always bordered with hydrangeas and pines, like a single endless garden with no other limit than the restraint and good education of the weekend citizens, owners of small chalets of wood and stone, each with its little dock and its boat, and their names: Small Retreat, The Calm, Rest Stop, My Refuge, My Hearth. Nowadays many of the gardens have been neglected, and the homes for which they were set up have been withdrawn to the background, resigned to being abandoned, adhering exclusively to the memory. In a progressive way, the city is living thus, suspended, floating over a fog that comes from the river and that will end by taking up residence in the whole area and by displacing the English spirit of the parks and the French elegance of the hotels and other buildings, until everything returns to the misty indistinguishableness of the estuary, to the winds and the loneliness.

Because the other face of the city is the wind. Every spring the wind blows in. When the calendar indicates springtime, it is a Lenten wind, and the people react to it with peculiar resentment, entrenching themselves inside, constantly shutting doors and windows. Nonetheless, it is never possible to avoid it completely. Always, at some time during the day, especially in the mornings, one finds it necessary to go out on the street, and then when least expected the wind rises with all the dust the city has accumulated, all the leaves thrown down so inopportunely by the trees, along with all sorts of filthy papers, trash, litter. It gets into one through the eyes, the nose, provoking a particular sort of agitation, an irritableness, an insecurity, an urge to get back home quickly to the protective cloister of the familiar walls. This is the wind of the city that has rejected water, that has expelled it from its enclosure perhaps through a fear—justified or not—of shipwreck or of being overwhelmed by that ambiguous liquidness, by the tremulous motion of canals: frightened by that other aspect of its nature that used to make it seem like Venice and that it has preferred to deny in order to keep with its austere look, its muffled beauty, its skin-deep dreariness that does not dare to slip, to take another step, to turn itself into an inner melancholy.

The wind can always be unpredictable, sharp and cutting as a whistle, pregnant with a freezing drizzle that is still trying to make winter eternal even when the start of summer has already announced its suffocating self. But that is in the other city, the one with the numerous parks and the river of undefined color, where the presence of water is the only element that seems a little bit wild and rustic, yet even so, not lacking in moderation, in a kind of harmony that has been foreseen and calculated.

And in the other city, drowsing on the edge of its sand dunes, where the only excess is absence, the absence of rain, of color, of vegetal life, the wind is absent as well, like the very air itself almost, snuffed out between the sky that is too low and the smutty grisaille of the flat roofs.

The wind is, finally, the northerly, or else a hurricane. When it is the northerly, it pierces giddily into the city, whipped on by the exaggerated waters that, following behind it, also push into the streets near the ocean. This is the cold wind that awakens a nostalgia for distant winters that have been forbidden this city. When it is a hurricane, it picks up everything the heat and light have buried, extracts it, passes it through more or less urban hiding places and then leaves it there, open to everyone's gaze, open to discovery. Always the wind is a longed-for disorder, the hope of an unforeseen mutation that might shatter, disturb, and cast turmoil into the everyday. The residents of this city love the wind.

The strange thing is that none of them knows the others exist, so close by, superimposed, as one might say; made of the same stuff, variants of an identical theme, attuned to different rhythms, a melody that was foreseen from the earliest times, from an epoch when the measuring of time was not needed because this was infinite and filled the world of mankind with its excessive wealth. Nothing was denied it, and everything belonged to it. Cities, therefore, when they started growing, still preserved a little of that splendor. They were born satisfied and brim full, believing that nothing would ever be stripped from them. They let themselves be painted in all colors, they accepted everything: balconies, columns, gratings, doorways, names. The numberless names that would take possession of them believing that this would be for always, not knowing that others would take their places, and then others again, until there was no one who recalled that first name, the name of its origins.

Nowadays it is difficult to know which was first. Which of all the cities is the true one. Even those that have a tendency to forget know that the one which shares something of the nature of the sea is always more. The rest, those that remain smothered among the mountains, crushed between the cordilleras, lost in the depths of the valleys, and too firmly anchored to the land, are made of dust and are like the dust: cities constructed over the dead and around the dead. But we must not forget that we are dealing with an artful device, because we are not speaking of different cities but of a single one, the very one that is at once generous and recondite, untidy and impeccable, Mediterranean and tropical, the one that is a mirage, a nostalgia, a lost echo, all at the same time, and, moreover, the only invention of fantasy with sufficient reality to be susceptible of being felt to the touch.

In the lithographs, looking frayed above a sky that occupies the largest part of the engraving, fragile figures wrapped in shawls get down from their buggies, their volantes, and stroll among the cypresses beside the meticulously sketched gas lights and lanterns of the Plaza de Armas, while the drivers, lingering and waiting, chat with women of color on the borders of the composition; on the seabank in the foreground, strolling vendors and stray dogs meet. This takes place not on the Plaza but in the Alameda de Paula. To the left, one after the other the houses repeat themselves, each with its single floor and its one high, narrow window protected by a grating of straight bars; and in the middle, between the houses and the sea, the empty esplanade, without a single tree that justifies the name of "Alameda," or

> ". . . the promenade, named after the famous one in Madrid, the Prado. The new Prado stretched a mile in length, a little more or less, forming an almost unnoticeable angle of 80 degrees in front of the little square where the rustic fountain of Neptune used to stand. It comprised four rows of trees common to Cuba's forests, some of them quite heavy with age and all of them inappropriate for an alameda, for an avenue lined with poplar trees."

Something unusual is beginning to take place: a resident of an old home in the old part of the city enters his house at night and goes to sleep; the following day, when he goes outside, he finds that some kind of modification difficult to pin down has taken place, a change that he could not describe—not even at that moment—seeing it as he does, because although he is looking right at it, this is not a change that has occurred on the surface but a little deeper within, from where it emanates and gradually emerges at different points, in little nuances, details, qualities that escape the preciseness of the word and that at most would even resist the pursuit of an adjective that is somewhat vague and generalizing. But what has all this to do with this man's going out, this resident of the old city, one morning on a day in the month of December, an exit that still has not taken place because precisely at the instant when he is about to set foot—the right one—over the threshold of the faded, splintered doorway, he has stumbled over uncertainty and surprise? It is easy to get lost in words. Nonetheless, one must make an effort to recall that words always, even in spite of ourselves, mean something. Is there anything other than these words that might attest to the "something unusual," the change, the modification taking place at that point in the old city on a December morning of this year? I could say that summer began without transition on that December day. The only proof is the vague and undefinable feeling of the man who thought of, who is thinking of leaving his house as he does every day. And this man, no matter how much I would like him to be, is not here to give his testimony. And even if he were, that testimony would be useless. Because this man, whom I have invented, would cease to have the slightest trace of the reality necessary to claim the right of existence if he should "really" find himself at this moment in any place away from this page, even though that place might be the threshold of the faded, splintered doorway of his house in the oldest part of the city.

Similar occurrences began to come to light on every side. The people were losing the concept of the seasons, the hours, the year marked by the calendar—that is, they were losing the notion of time. That was when they conjointly began to lose their own identity, the moment when some of them, becoming desperate, gave themselves over to the whim of exhibitng personal objects, especially watches, as a guarantee or the ultimate pledge of a personal existence that was now felt to be gone astray or on the verge of being lost. Some began to get old articles of clothing out of their trunks that had not had contact with the air for perhaps half a century or more. They contemplated them with astonishment and the enthusiasm of children who have just received a new toy or of savages delighted with the colored beads they have just obtained in exchange for something much more valuable (from the point of view of civilized people). There were those who succeeded in using them, in dressing in them, and even in going out on the street in them, swearing that they had nothing else to put on and that they would prefer these antiquated but elegant garments to the impersonal, frayed, colorless wear that was usual in those times. It happened, then, that many people were suddenly running into those images from another century right in the middle of the street and, quite disturbed, they were starting to be affected themselves, starting to check over their own clothing wide-eyed, ready to think that, indeed, an odd change had taken place overnight and that it must have been fifty, sixty, or seventy years ago—according to the person—that what was happening this very day, this month, this year, at the very hours, minutes, and seconds marked on their watches, was taking place, etc., etc., etc.

> *"The young Cubans, the Creoles, considered it be-*
> *neath them to appear on the Prado afoot, above all to*
> *mingle with the Spaniards in the lines of Sunday*

spectators. So that only the most important people took an active part in the promenade; women, invariably in their buggies, some older people in volantes, and a few young men of rich families on horseback. No other kinds of carriages were in use then in Havana. . . . The greater the affluence of the latter, the smaller the latitude wherein they were permitted to move, the result often being a rather monotonous exercise, a situation which in truth was not wasted on the girls, whose principal amusement consisted in searching out their friends and acquaintances among the spectators in the side streets and greeting them with half-open fans in that gracious and elegant manner which is given only to the women of Havana."

But one has to go still further back to arrive at the origins; back to the beginnings, where all possibilities and non-possibilities were still gathered together without differentiating them, above all that of death, so very close to that of being something only by half, indistinct and ambiguous, a primary lack of organization; back to the disorder from which the structure of the city (no one then existed who might put it on record) still might or might not be able to rise.

To rise:

cathedrals multiplied to infinity in prisms of light; screens; arched windows; women with their long, vegetal locks; fruits heaped on oval trays in the middle of the table, in the middle of rooms suspended in midair, dangling from light broken up into the colors of the rainbow (from the stained-glass windows) and all the rounded, curved, twisted lines, balconies, window gratings everywhere, faces . . . All the images that have been fixed on canvases, the designs that have been recovered, such as that chair, all by itself, surrounded by woodland profusion, painted by Lam and preserved on the white wall of a drawing room, the drawing room of the novelist, the one that has done precisely that: lay out forms, outline boundaries around the indefinite, and reconstitute things (by means of a journey that does not involve going back to the seed) that would have been about to disappear: textures; marble, always under threat from heat, tile, and plaster; dense odors and sounds. Is it possible to distinguish them?

The city is
> *... the endless street with its four streetcar tracks, the cables on a level with the balconies, those white-and-yellow, yellow-and-white balconies, the white-or-black iron balconies repeating themselves to infinity along that street.*

The city is what surrounds the house:
> *... with a murmuring so hoarse, or sharp, or sibilant, like the crackling of a huge bonfire sometimes, perhaps the sound of the sun as it burns the rocks, a vibration that beats in the outside air and that tries to assault the walls and blinds, tries to slip into the protected shadows where ...*

It is the wall:
> *... the wall separating the street from the rocks and the sea.*

The city is the sea
> *... that is all around, so near.*

And the wind
> *. . . always . . .*

It is also
> *. . . a huge corrugated mollusk that has never completely left the sea.*

And the arcades that
> *. . . were empty.*

The columns
> *. . . with capitals Ionic and Doric, with acanthus leaves, all honeycombed by the saltpeter . . .*

Sensations:
> *. . . a creeping, faltering tension that slips in through the doors and windows so uselessly opened in order to see if it is raining.*

The gardens that, as their usual habit,
> *. . . had a lamentable, almost pathetic aspect.*

And which are always distant, inaccessible gardens. But above all, there has been, there is, and there will be the rain:
> *. . . soft, light, almost furtive; unhurried, calm; heavier, stronger, happier; thick and imperturbable; hurried, stentorian, and violent; indiscriminate, loud and obvious, careless and devastating.*

The advantage is that all of this, what the city is in these words, has a certain likelihood of assuring it, no matter what happens, some kind of survival. There is no other remedy than to enclose it with words. To build a wall of words around it that will forever take the place of the other wall that tried to keep it safe and only half-way managed to do so. Words have this advantge over brick and stone: neither the pick nor the erosive labor of the elements is capable of demolishing them or sweeping them away. Therefore it is necessary to go on searching for words: words that siphon off something of its being from the city in order to deposit this in a safe place, as invulnerable as the pages of a book can be (or can they?), any book at all; words that give us back—enclosed within the confines that it possessed, has possessed, or possesses at some moments—the city, a rag of its slippery importance, a tatter of its evanescent nature.

Words:

> "... *strangely, at this hour of reverberations and long shadows, like a huge baroque chandelier whose glass facets, green, red, orange, give color to a disordered rubble of balconies, arcades, cupolas, belvederes, and galleries of shutters ...*"
>
> "... *those natural terraces that history has made into a park that I always confuse with its twin Avenue of the Presidents ...*"
>
> "... *Poseidon, this Neptune that in Cuba has avenues and statues and streetlamps ... The street ... begins in the Central Park.*"
>
> "... *in the shadow of the trees (laurels or false laurels, jacarandas, flamboyant when in bloom, and, in the distance, the enormous ficuses in the park that are split in two by the path and I never can remember what their name is and where those giants come from that look like a single Bo Tree repeated in a blasphemous game of mirrors) with crowns and when we arrived at the pines, nearer to the coast ..., the smell of the sea ...*"
>
> "*The huge leaves of the banana tree looked as though*

*they were rocking a newborn baby. I saw a poinciana
that looked like a mollusk with its valves in the morning; it was full of cocuyo beetles."*

Because the city, mine as well as theirs, is a beam of
light that suddenly scatters to become lost in the rugged
pathways of the night. Its rhythm is buried, obscure, like that
of a huge woody copse surrounded by ocean echoes. In the
middle of that hollow lies its beginning and its end. All the
words, up to now, have known only how to surround that
intimate circle of silence. Is memory really futile?

*The hot and burning city was only an unreal city, the
imagined city of a mirage.**

---

*The texts that appear in italics plus quotation marks come from the following authors and
books: Cirilo Villaverde, CECILIA VALDES; Alvaro de la Iglesia, TRADICIONES CUBANAS;
Alejo Carpentier, EL SIGLO DE LAS LUCES; Guillermo Cabrera Infante, TRES TRISTES
TIGRES; José Lezama Lima, PARADISO. The texts that appear in italics without quotation
marks have been selected by the author from other texts of hers, some of them included in this
book, others in the novel MUERTE POR AGUA.